CU00854012

Vampire – Child of

by Charmain Marie Mitchell

Publisher: CMMpublishing, Petersfield, UK, GU32 3NF

First published in the UK, US, & worldwide 2013
Edition Two

ISBN-13:
978-1495313042
ISBN-10:
1495313042

www.charmainmariemitchell.com

I dedicate this book to my beautiful children, William, Jesse, Bonnie, and Ben, because all children have an amazing destiny.

I would like to thank my partner Mike, for his continued encouragement and support during the writing of this book. I would also like to thank to my four gorgeous children, and my lovely parents.

Lastly, a huge thank you to Julia Gibbs, better known as juliaproofreader, for her proofreading services – great as always.

Contents

Vampire - Child of Destiny

Chapter One

2013

Once again, I take up my pen and recall the memories from my long life. It has been a while since I have attempted to write. Writing the first chapters of my life affected me much more than I could ever have known, and for weeks after I finished writing, I awoke at night screaming in terror, the sound of my baby's cries echoing around my muddled mind.

I have therefore been afraid to write! I have several times picked up my pen, but before my thoughts have been able to string together the first sentence, I have put my pen back down on my writing desk and walked away, my fear following me like a gliding poisonous snake.

Oh, I am sure you read this with a mind that questions my writing, after all the entire whole world knows that vampires have no emotions and are evil creatures, do they not? Oh, if only that was the truth! How so much easier my life would be.

How strange it is that I recall my first memories with a young heart and not that of a mind and body that has lived for nearly five hundred years. I had thought that reliving my memories through an aged and wise mind would make them so much easier to deal with, but of course, no matter how old we are, we never truly know the answers to all the questions we ask.

It seems that in reliving my memories I have also once again found an affinity with the human race. I had lost that. I saw people as food, but since revisiting my past I have remembered how it feels to be human, to be scared, alone, and above all petrified of the animal that I had unwillingly become.

I made this discovery a few days after I had finished writing. Actually, it was the morning following my first terror-induced nightmare. I was strolling barefoot along the soft warm sand at Pevensey Bay, a small and secluded beach near Brighton.

I love the ocean, it is the one thing in my long life that never changed, for the ocean can never be tamed, nor altered, and I find I constantly feel the need to be close to the sound of crashing waves.

After walking for a while, I decided to sit down and look out to sea; watching the waves was hypnotic and eased the remaining fear from the previous night's terror. I was so lost in thought that I failed to notice the young boy walking towards me, and it was not until the gorgeously intoxicating smell of fresh innocent blood assaulted my senses, that I knew he was almost upon me.

I hate to admit that in years gone by I would have fed from this child. The taste of young untainted blood is irresistible. It regenerates the decrepit blood that circulates in a very old vampire's body, eradicating all the sourness of the immoral beings previously fed from, and replenishes us with youth and vitality. I suppose in some ways, like humans, eating a healthy but delicious diet; that is what an innocent's blood is to a vampire.

I felt my fangs grow as the boy approached me, the sweet smell of his life engulfing my senses. I wanted his blood, and I knew at that moment that my eyes had glazed over with the familiar opaque look of a crazed animal, my fangs had elongated and that I looked like the beast that I had long ago become. I jumped up from my seated position, my body fighting an internal battle, my mind screaming, 'NO' but my body craving the elixir of the boy's blood.

I then did something that I had not done for centuries. I fled! I knew I could no longer feed on the blood of one so young, and for the first time in years, I felt disgust at the want of my desires.

For miles, I scurried along the coastline, I say scurried because I feel that I was no better than a rat. Rats infect the innocent with a plague of death and debauchery, and I believe this is also an apt description of a vampire.

Finally, I come to rest miles away from the boy and bury myself away from human gaze underneath Brighton pier. I writhe with the agony of self-loathing on the damp sand, pathetic, self-pitying sobs shaking my body.

Gradually the sobs subside, but it is then that I taste the presence of a human nearby. I glance to my side and notice an old man curled up on the wet sand. His hands lovingly holding an empty wine bottle as if it was a precious stone and although his body smelt like death, his soft snores proved he lived. The yearning for blood once more took over my body, but this time it was different, this was not innocence – this was food.

I grasped the man and sunk my teeth into his neck. My thirst was so angry and intense that I did not stop until I ceased to hear the irregular beats of his failing heart, but then I flung him from me in disgust and his poor misused body fell in a crumpled heap. The pickled taste of his alcohol-infused blood stung my throat, and bending over, I retched and retched, until black cloying clots colored the sand at my feet.

I flung myself on the man's body. He was

dead, I knew he was dead, but I tried to feed him my blood, I needed to bring him back to life, to undo the evil I had done.

"*Please breathe!*" I screamed to the wind. Sobs once again rasped from my throat, but to no avail. I knew that I was not going to be able to return to him what I had stolen. This man was not innocent, but he was defenseless, and I had taken his one magical gift, in what was a miserable existence, I had taken his life!

Wearily I returned to my home, I was so close to stabbing a stake deep into my unfeeling heart. Thoughts of death rushed in a crazy spiral around my dazed mind. For hours I lay on my bed, a wooden stake held in my hand beside me. Several times, I held it above my chest; several times I came close to letting it fall into my breast.

However, slowly a realisation came to me - I felt guilt. For the first time, in a long time I felt a human emotion. Maybe, just maybe, I am worth saving. Maybe I did have a reason to live. Yes, I had selfishly taken a human life, and there was no excuse, but now, just maybe, I could find a reason to live? The guilt I felt, a feeling that would remain with me, was a human reaction, and as long as I felt that guilt, I knew I would not be able to take another human life.

I pulled my journal towards me and started to read. When I had finished I closed my eyes with a sigh, and I knew I would continue with the tale of my long life, it was a story that needed to be told. I needed the world to know the truth, and I needed to know the truth, because for the first time in a long time, I was finding Gwen - the real me.

So once more, we begin...

Part One

Chapter Two

1542

Robert softly enters my bedchamber; even with the velvet drapes drawn around the bed, I know it is he. Although I am a young, inexperienced, and newly transformed vampire, my senses are astronomical when compared to when I was human.

Sights, smells, feelings, everything is so much more intense. Colours are brighter, life is sweeter, and in fact, just everything is amazing. My senses are now so finely tuned, that I recognise Robert by the sound of his tread, his breathing, even the faint taste of his scent that seems to float on the air. I have the intoxicating feeling of invincibility, and although I am in truth dead, I have never felt so alive.

"Boo!" Robert's head appears around the curtain, his smile, as always, hypnotic and mesmerizing.

"I knew it was you!" I said, poking my

tongue out, and faking disdain by turning my back on him. "Oh, did you indeed?" Although my back was to him, I could hear the smile in his voice. The bed dipped as he climbed in beside me, I could feel his cold breath on my neck, and my body trembled in response to him.

"Well," Robert whispered into my ear, "Did you know I was going to do this?" His tongue slivered a delicious line along my neck. "Or this?" His voice deepened as he pierced my skin with his elongated and exquisite fangs. I sighed in ecstasy; nothing could have ever prepared me for the exquisite feeling of making love with a vampire. The giving and receiving of blood, two bodies entwined, emotionally and physically, combined with the heightened awareness of being a vampire, arousing emotions that can only be described, quite hypocritically, as heavenly. I had voiced this thought to Robert a few days earlier, and he had laughed his deep throaty laugh, and said, "Oh but thou knoweth not what thou sayeth!"

"And my love, did you know I was going

to do this?" Robert asked as he thrust his body into mine. I screamed with joy, and joined him in our mutual pleasure, love, life, blood, and power, building into a climax of ecstasy.

A few hours later, lying in Roberts's arms, my pleasure still sweet but fading, I asked him the question that I had asked him every day since I had become a vampire.

"Can I see him today?" His sigh answered my question before he had even voiced it. "She'll not allow it, Gwen." I jumped out of the bed. I had known that he would answer me in this way, no matter how I asked, begged, and cried, his answer was always the same. I paced the bedchamber, irritation causing my movements to feel aggravated and clumsy. I turned to face Robert, anger visible in my stance and the blaze of my eyes. "But why not? He is my son, Robert!"

He remained quiet, watching me as I paced up and down, his eyes, as always, lazy and unconcerned. "Because, Gwen," he said quietly, "Because you agreed that

Henry would become Matilda's child."

I once again stopped my pacing, which I had resumed, and turned towards him. "But he is *her* child! That's quite clear, is it not.....I have not even seen him, I have not seen my *SON,* I just want to see him, to touch him, surely that is understandable...Please, Robert, Please..."

He arose from the bed and walked, gloriously beautiful and naked, towards me. "The maternal bond must be broken, Gwen. I have explained this to you countless times." His hand reached out to me, I shrugged him away angrily, and he sighed, dropping his hand down by his side. "In a few months' time you will be able to see him, and maybe even play with him...but...until then you must allow Matilda and Henry to bond."

His eyes glanced at me in a cold stare, stern and unyielding, and I knew that his look signaled the end of the conversation. I would not be able to convince him today and in truth, I knew I would never convince him, no matter how much I begged. I had made a bargain with him before our love had grown, and before my son was born, and I knew Robert would never break that bargain.

"But I am your lover, Robert! You share your body with me every night, you spend your days with me...Matilda is nothing to you...and is your wife only in name..."
"That, for the moment, is true. However, do not presume to know how I feel about Matilda! Matilda will always be my wife, and it is well that you remember that, because it will never change, you will never be that, now or ever! I am sorry, Gwen, but that is how it is!"

I noticed the compassion etched into his face, but I was too angry to care. "Well, that being the case, sir," I said, my voice full of sarcasm and anger, "I recommend that you had best go and sleep in your wife's arms, for I'll not be a doxy for you tonight!"

His compassionate expression faded, replaced instantly by anger, and as his eyes grew red, I wondered if I had indeed pushed him too far. I had seen his wrath in the past, and having witnessed him kill several vampires a few months previously when I was a human, it was not something, I would, in all truth, look forward to seeing again. I waited expectantly for the cruel punishment I thought I was going to receive. Instead of expressing his anger in this, he simply bowed towards me, walked to the bed, snatched up his clothes, and said, on his way to the door, "As you wish, my lady."

Anger washed over me. How could he do this to me? I flung myself down on the bed, rage running like poison through my body, curses flowing from my lips. I knew deep down that I should not expect him to act in any other way. He was, after all, the man who killed the father of my child and all of his family. He was the man who had given me the choice of living and giving my unborn son up to him and his wife, or dying and condemning my unborn child to death. He was the man who had stolen my life, in every sense of the word, and in doing so condemned me to an eternity of depravity. How could I be so stupid to believe that this man, this man whom I loved, and who I believed loved me, would ever let anyone or anything stand in the way of what he wanted?

My rage subsided, but it was rapidly replaced by sorrow, as my mind relived the last few months. The residual human part of me recoiled and grimaced with terror at the horrors I had witnessed. The new, vampire element, accepted that everything I had seen was part of my new life, and the fact of the matter was that I needed to accept my life as it was now.

Rising from the bed, I walked to the door, and ushered in the serving girl Anne whom I had heard rushing down the corridor. Leading her to the bed, I bade her sit down, and then taking her slim wrist into my hand I bit gently into her thin translucent skin. The taste of her salty but sweet blood eased my mind further, and I felt myself drift into the realms of beauty, which a vampire shares with their victim. Floating in this world of bliss I heard a soft voice ask, "But what does the Gwen part of you think?" and I heard my inner voice scream with venom, "Gwen needs revenge!"

Chapter Three

Anne left my bedchamber looking pale and wane, and although I hated the fact that I needed to drink blood to survive, I felt sated and vibrantly alive after feeding from her. I had decided whilst feasting on Anne that I needed to make my own way in this new world. I wanted two things: My son, and to gain revenge, and I was not going to get either by begging Robert.

I was going to take what was mine, but not yet. I had made a promise to myself that when Henry was old enough I would attempt to flee Vanike and Robert, taking him with me. However, for now the time was not right, Henry was too young to survive and more importantly, I was not strong enough to protect him.

I had eighteen years to achieve this feat, for I would never accept the fact that my son would grow to manhood simply to become a vampire. Robert had stated, when we made our bargain, that Henry would be reborn as a vampire on his eighteenth birthday, and on this day, he would become a prince amongst vampires. I did not want my son to become a prince amongst vampires! I wanted him to have a normal life, free from murder and evil, but wanting this for him was dangerous. If Robert caught me even sneaking to see Henry then I would face at least banishment or even death. For myself I did not care, but if I failed then I would fail my son, and that I could not do. I had been searching for a way to see my child, but I had so far been unable to sneak past Matilda's women, but I had decided that I would bide my time and that I would eventually succeed.

My words may have been strong, but in truth, I bled inside. The need to see my son grew stronger every day. I imagined his chubby face, and his sweet smile, for I feel certain he would be smiling by now. Henry was ripped from my slashed womb to enable him to live, and as I died, I heard his cry, and rejoiced that he lived, but not once did I see his face. Matilda had whisked him away, certain that I was dead, but Robert had fed me his blood, and against all the odds, I had survived. I was certain I had survived so that my son could live his life without their depravity, for as much as I loved Robert, he lived an evil existence, and I did not intend to give my son up to his will.

I decided I would no longer beg Robert for a glimpse of my son. I would act as if I accepted his words, and that I no longer cared for the child of my heart. I would also go out of my way to find friendship amongst the vampires. I needed their trust to be able to move freely around the manor, and to gain their trust, I needed to show them I had fully embraced my new life.

I walked over to the chest that housed my gowns. Tonight I needed to show Robert I had accepted his command, and so I chose my most alluring gown. Becoming a vampire had changed my appearance. My dark hair, once straight and sometimes lifeless, now hung around my shoulders in glittering curls, vibrant and beautiful. My eyes, which had always been my best feature, now not only shone with mischief, but with a blue brilliance to rival any sapphire. My lips shone red like cherries, and my figure had returned to that of a maiden. I had noticed, several times, the eyes of some of the male vampires following me lustfully, while the women's eyes glittered with jealousy. I had not yet taken advantage of my new beauty, and now was the time to start.

I quickly stepped into my blue dress, deciding for the first time ever that I had no need of a chemise or a corset, and I laced my bodice tightly to ensure that my breasts showed to great advantage. I then pulled my stomacher tightly to enhance the appearance of my small waist, and I left my hair to fall down my back like a shimmering cape.

No sooner had I started down the stairs, which led to the grand hall, than several pairs of eyes followed by progress. Stares burned into my skin, but I noticed no one, my eyes were searching for just one man.

Robert was sprawled in a large chair near the fire, his hands full of a newly transformed vampire called Emily. Jealousy pierced my heart, but I refused to give in to my emotions, and instead looked towards a vampire called Louis who was lounging on the bottom step, lazily but hungrily watching my movements, desire stamped on his face. Louis was, as his name suggested, French. "Bonjour, mademoiselle," he said bowing low. "Bonjour, Louis," I laughed, as he grasped my hand in his, lowering his mouth to kiss my hand. "You are very beautiful tonight, mademoiselle...maybe too beautiful, huh?" His eyes shifted in the direction of Robert. I followed his gaze, and almost gasped from the piercing ray of rage that radiated from Robert's eyes. Robert's hands were still full of Emily, who sat facing him on his lap, her legs twisted around his body, but his eyes were full of me, and he was not happy!

I turned back to Louis and said, "Please excuse me, Louis, I wish to move closer to the fire." Louis chuckled, "Of course, ma petite...I also have no wish to die tonight, huh? He bowed lower over my hand, and whispered, "Lord Robert...is um, a little put out...do not make him too angry, mademoiselle." I smiled towards Louis, but my eyes never once left Robert's. Mesmerized by his angry stare, and bound by the fierceness in his eyes, I moved closer towards him, but it was more than that, I felt transfixed by him, by his desire for me.

I stopped in the middle of the great hall and continued to watch him. He smiled, but it was twisted and angry, and I knew that he was going to do something to punish me. A chill ran up and down my spine, and I knew that I had been stupid to test Robert's love for me. I had angered him, and someone was going to suffer.

I watched, stunned, as his fangs grew and his head flung back, then snapped forward and then proceeded to rip Emily's throat out. Shrieks of excitement circled the great hall as Robert held her limp body high above him with outstretched hands, his mouth and front smeared and swamped with dripping blood.

A sigh of relief escaped my throat in a soft hiss as he threw her body on the huge table; I thought he intended to let her heal, how wrong I was! Like a flash of lightening, he threw one of the long but thin logs that were stacked beside the fire.

His aim was straight and true, piercing Emily's heart with a sickening thud, and so ended her newly transformed vampire life. I did not vomit and I did not move, I just stood quietly, waiting for him to reach my side. I drowned out the sound of the evil nest of vipers surrounding me, their cheers at the death of one of their own sickening and cruel.

He reached my side in a flash, his presence consumed me, and his whisper caused me to shake. "You see how easily I can take away all that I have given you, my love." Grabbing my waist, he swung me around in a circle, his laughter and the laughter of the other vampires around him echoed around my head without gaiety, and I knew in that moment that he would most definitely kill me if I ever abused his trust.

Chapter Four

Robert's eyes shifted rapidly around the crowd of vampires, his eyes shone with excitement and malice. He looked down at me, a cruel and spiteful smile playing around his soft and gorgeous lips.

Letting go of my hand, he jumped gracefully onto the huge table, which still housed the dead body of Emily. He walked over to her body, and casually, with no emotion or regret, kicked her body from the table. The crowd of vampires once more laughed and shrieked, and I felt disgust for their depravity overwhelm me.

Robert lifted his hand to hush the crowd. "My friends...shh, my friends..." he waited patiently for the crowd to quiet, and when he had their attention, he continued, "My friends, I have a treat for you." He smiled down at them, and if I had any doubt before, his presence, and their reaction to him, confirmed that he was their king, and the leader of them all.

"Tonight we will have a live dinner." I gasped in horror, but the other vampires cheered and heckled in glee. I was not sure what he meant by 'a live dinner' and I was sure that I really did not want to know.

"We also have a treat for our newly transformed vampire, Gwen." Robert's face shone evilly, his laughter, spite, and anger, radiating towards me in waves. He had, I knew, decided to punish me for my earlier outburst in the bedchamber. "Gwen will have the honor of making her first kill." His red eyes shone into mine, and I know that he saw the horror I felt at his words. Clapping his hands in what resembled childish glee, he shouted over the crowd of crazed animals, "*BRING IN THE FEAST!*"

All heads, including mine, turned towards the curtain that hid the entrance to the kitchens at the far end of the great hall. Four naked people walked from the entrance, I could see from the glazed and faraway expressions on their face that they had been bewitched.

I did not recognise three of them, but the fourth I did, it was my maid, Anne, and I knew without being told, that she was the one that Robert had decided I would feed from until she was starved of blood and her heart stopped beating.

I watched the four of them make their way to the table. The excitement of the other vampires faded from my mind, because all I could see and hear were the four innocent people climbing onto the table. The sight of the four of them, artfully arranging themselves in preparation for their own deaths, was truly hideous and revolting!

Robert jumped from the table, landing beside me. I could tell from the sardonic quirk of his mouth that he could tell that I felt disgusted by what I was witnessing. My compassion, the one thing he had always told me he loved best about me, was the one emotion that he was now using against me. For the first time I was seeing the man who slaughtered Tom's family so heartlessly, and it was a man that I hated!

I wanted to run away and definitely did not want to take Anne's life. Feeding from a human was one thing, but stealing life from the innocent was not my idea of fun. I thought it barbaric and cruel. However, I knew that if I refused to do as Robert commanded then he would become angrier, and whilst he was in a rage like this, I was not sure that if I disobeyed him, I would or would not be lying on the floor in a heap like Emily.

I felt his gaze searing into my flesh as he waited to see how I would react. I also felt the crowd's eyes on me; they were all waiting to see how I would take this command. It was a test. A test I really did not want to partake in, but I knew that I would need to perform it, before I gained their trust.

I am certain that Robert saw the emotions play across my face, he knew how I was feeling, but he would not give in, it was my turn to submit. "Come, my love," he whispered, "Our feast awaits..."

A solitary tear made its way down my cheek as I looked up at him. He lifted his hand and gently wiped the tear away with his thumb, and then whilst his eyes burnt into mine, his tongue darted out, licking the salty proof of my compassion. Leading me closer to the table, he said, "Your tears are mine, your life is mine, you are mine...never forget that!"

Shaking my hand from his grip, I walked towards Anne. I wanted to get this finished as quickly as possible. I knew the others would play with their victims for hours, teasing, and torturing them, but I just could not do that.

Looking into Anne's guileless, innocent eyes, tears once again fell from my eyes. Leaning forward, I gently swept the hair from her face and neck. "I'm so sorry, please forgive me," I whispered. Her answering smile, I knew, would become a bittersweet memory for many years to come.

My fangs sunk deep into her jugular. The taste of her blood, although in truth exquisite; would always be remembered as bitter. I drank deeply, willing her to die quickly.

Her body became limp in my arms, her skin cold to the touch. I heard the soft fluttering of her heart, attempting to pump a substance that no longer flowed so freely through her body. THUMP...THUMP...Then, nothing.

I pulled my fangs from her neck, and looked into her pale lifeless face. I knew the other vampires would think I was pathetic, but not caring what they thought, I once again gently stroked her hair into place. This time I covered the evidence of the puncture wounds I had made whilst taking her young innocent life. I did not care what they thought anymore. I wished I had resisted, even if that had meant Robert's wrath.

I sensed Robert move behind me, and I gently lay Anne back on the table. I closed her eyes with my fingertips, and then turned towards Robert. "It needed to be done, my love...you needed to let go." His voice had returned to a soft and gentle tone, his face shone with empathy for my pain. "Did it?" I said, my voice ringing angrily in my ears. "Don't you have enough followers, enough murderers. any of these," I swung my arms around to indicate the vampires surrounding us, "Would kill for you...but that's not enough is it? You collect souls, Robert. However, I assure you of this; no matter how many people you order me to kill, you will never own my soul... NOT NOW, *NOT EVER*!"

I yanked my arm from his hand, and although I heard some of the vampires gasp, I was unconcerned. Anger returned to his face, but I was beyond worrying about that, and hissed, "Kill me if you wish, Robert, torture me, hate me...I don't care, but you will never succeed in ordering me to kill an innocent person ever again!"

I pushed through the crowd, ignoring their stares, grins, and hissing voices. I probably would be dead by this time tomorrow, without ever laying eyes on my son. My son, whom I now knew, more than ever, would not be able to remain here, reared by animals, only to become a beast. Well if I die, so be it, but if I lived, I would make sure, one way or another, to save my son from the destiny Robert had predicted for him.

Chapter Five

Lying on my bed, I heard sounds of merriment from the great hall float on the air, and I felt sickened by the cause of the merriment. I had been so angry when I had reached my bedchamber that I had not even bothered to get undressed, and instead flung myself face down on the bed, my fist occasionally hitting the bed covering in rage.

I knew that Robert would soon seek me out, his anger threatening and lethal, but I had resigned myself to whatever fate befell me. I was not angry with Robert, I was angry with myself. Angry, that I had allowed myself to murder Anne.

I must have fallen asleep, because I awoke to find the candle had burnt itself out, and the air was still with silence. Instantly, I knew that Robert had entered the room, his aroma, his presence, surrounded me. I sat up in bed, looking for him in the darkness.

"Are you looking for me, by any chance?" His voice echoed just inches from my ear, causing me to jump. "No...No, I wasn't...I heard a noise, that was all." His chuckle sent shivers down my spine. The sound indicated he was in a good mood, but with Robert, I could never be too sure. "Are you afraid of me, Gwen?" he whispered. "No! No, I'm not," I stammered, then continued, "I'm not a mouse to your cat, Robert, if you want to hurt or kill me, then just do so!" Again, he chuckled, and then suddenly, without warning, he thrust me back on the bed, his body on top of mine, his hands holding mine down. "You have no idea what you do to me do you, Gwen? I could have killed you tonight, and I would have done so, if it had been anyone else."

My eyes had grown accustomed to the dark and I could now see his gaze, his eyes intense, circled by an amber light. "If you loved me you wouldn't have made me kill Anne," I spat out. "I did not make you kill Anne, you made that decision yourself. You could have said no, but you did not."

He was right, I could have said no! His words repeated inside my head repeatedly, whipping me with their harshness. "You're right...I killed her..." Pain sliced through me, shaking my body with its force. "*I KILLED HER!*" I screamed out with an inner rage directed only at myself.

Roberts hold on me tightened, the more I screamed, the tighter he held. Finally, my sobs and anger subsided and I felt numb and limp from the guilt that coursed through my body. I had taken a life!

"I'm sorry, Gwen, but you needed to know your own strength, to know how far you can go. In future you will take more lives, I'm sure of it, but there will be justified reasons." I shook my head, knowing I would never take another life. Robert chuckled, "I promise that one day you will, but this memory will prepare you for the future."
"I don't believe you, Robert! Yes, I think you thought I needed to take a life, but you were also punishing me...I know you

were." His eyes shone with love, but I heard the catch in his voices as he said, "You know me too well, my love." He then paused for a moment. I knew him well enough to know that he was contemplating his next words carefully. "I was jealous! I saw you gliding down the stairway. Every eye taking in your perfection and that damned Louis talking to you with lust in his gaze!"

Pouncing to a standing position, with anger in his stance, he turned from me and started pacing. "*I wanted to kill him*!" he growled in a low menacing voice, "But of course, I could not, *I wanted to kill you*, but of course I would never do such a thing. My heart twisted in my chest and so I took Emily to appease my anger..."

He stood at the foot of the bed and I could feel rage radiating from him. "But that wasn't enough," he whispered, anguish in his voice, "And so I goaded you into taking the life of Anne! I knew it was going to hurt you. I knew it, but I wanted to punish you."

Roberts head dropped to his chest and his

next words were a whispered plea, "Will you forgive me, Gwen, and will you still love me?" His words pierced my heart. How could I love a man who had so little regard for life?   Nevertheless, I did.   I opened my arms to him, and my gesture needed no words.   I loved him, and nothing would change that.

My mouth sought his in hunger. Robert gasped as I bit into his full lips, his blood trickling into both of our mouths, his bite piercing my tongue, our blood and tongues mingled in mind-numbing pleasure. We joined, a perfect union, sharing love, our bodies moving in a timeless rhythm, sharing our blood with bittersweet bites of passion.

"I love you, Gwen." Robert whispered. His hands tangled in my hair, my head resting lazily on his chest, both sleepy from our lovemaking. "I love you too," I replied, "very much!" I added.

I was on the verge of falling asleep, my thoughts wandering, drifting in and out of reality, when suddenly, I said aloud, "If you love me so much, why still deny me my son?" I knew I had made a mistake as soon as the words slipped from my mouth. Robert pushed me abruptly from him. "So we're back to this, are we?"

"I'm sorry, Robert...I did not mean...I really should not have... I did not mean to say that..." "So why say it? Did you say you loved me to try to persuade me? *Did you, Gwen*?" "Don't be ridiculous, Robert...I love you, you know I do!"

His face suddenly looked old, his eyes were old as time and held so many secrets, but suddenly they shone near to the surface, and I think, for the first time I saw the real Robert. He sat at the foot of the bed. His head drooped into his hands. "I love you, Gwen," he said, his voice so low that I needed to lean further towards him to ensure I heard him clearly. "I love you; I have not loved like this for a very long time...in fact centuries upon centuries." He had paused, but I waited for him to resume his mumbling, I did not want to interrupt him and stop the words I so wanted to hear. "I made the wrong choice once before, Gwen. A choice that I should not have made and it changed both of our lives forever. I betrayed someone I loved, and in doing so I changed everything forever!"

A strangled sob arose up through his throat, the sound akin to an animal in agony. "I see Henry's destiny, Gwen. I see it clearly, and he will be strong, and I cannot fail him, I cannot put love before duty again. I will not!" Finally, his eyes rose to meet mine. His sorrow reached out to me. "So you see, Gwen, no matter how much I love you, you ask me the one thing I cannot give you...I'm sorry, but I cannot, not now, not ever!"

I turned from him. His words told me he would never relent, no matter what I did, he was never going to change his mind, and I knew, likewise, I was never going to give in or change my mind. It was then that I knew that at some time in the future we would become enemies, because I could never forsake my son, and I knew, neither could Robert!

I was so weak compared to him, but I knew that one day I would fight him, and I knew that tomorrow I would start that fight. Robert did not know, he expected me to simply accept his command, but this time, he was mistaken.

I opened my arms to him, and we embraced, my words of comfort echoing around the bedchamber. However, my mind did not hear the words of comfort, although I uttered them. My mind was already processing and planning how I was going to get my son back.

Chapter Six

For week upon week, I tried to figure out the best way to see my son, but all of my ideas proved to be fruitless. The one thing I knew for sure was that he was housed in the south tower, but I quickly realised that there was not any way to get into the tower except by direct access through Matilda's bedchamber.

I had taken to walking towards the tower every day. I walked around and around the base, foolishly wishing that an opening would suddenly appear as if by magic. I would lean against the cold stone, hoping to hear the sounds of my child and sometimes I could swear that I heard him, but, of course, I couldn't be sure, and in reality, I think I knew that I was imagining that which I wanted to hear.

It was on a day such as this, when as I returned from my daily walk from the areas surrounding the tower, I felt someone snatch me from behind and I was pulled into a small alcove that was nestled in the tower wall. "Shh, mademoiselle, it is I, Louis. I wish to talk to you...please do not scream!" I yanked myself out of his arms, and turned towards him, my voice a whispered hiss. "What the hell do you think you're doing?" I asked him the question, but did not wait for him to answer and continued. "*You fool*, don't you know that Robert would kill you if he knew you laid hands on me?" "Oui, I know of this..." His head dropped to his chest, reminding me of a disobedient child, he continued. "I watch you...here every day...mademoiselle, it is sad and I wish to help you." "How can *you* help me, Louis?" I said in exasperation, "You're putting us both in danger by waylaying me..."

I gazed at him as if he was mad for a moment, and then turned away, intending to walk away. He grabbed my arm, swinging me back around to face him.

"I will help you, mademoiselle. I will help you rescue your petite garcon, if you will allow this?" "How do you intend to do that?" I said. "I have...how you say?" he asked me, a frown on his face. He then smiled, and continued, "I have made friends with his nurse...she will help us, ma petite...if you wish it?"

I was young, but not so young that I did not know that Louis would want something in return. "Why would you help me and place your life in danger?" I asked him, watching him carefully, noting a sly smile stirring behind his thin lips.

"I desire you, ma petite..." he reached his hand out to my face and ran his finger tentatively down my cheek. My instant reaction was to pull back from him in disgust, thus revealing that I felt sickened by his touch. "Aw, ma petite, you do not feel the same way, oui?" I remained silent, neither, confirming or denying his suspicion. Louis continued, "No matter, you will!" He bowed towards me, and then abruptly turned and walked away.

I was so confused! I knew that I would need Louis' help if I was going to see and escape with Henry, but the thought of him touching me, well, I just could not comprehend such a thing. I loved Robert, I was sure of that, but it seemed that Louis' help was the only way I was able, for the foreseeable future, to get my son back. I really did not know what to do, and I knew that if Robert found out, he would kill us both.

The decision I needed to make became an agonizing one, I wanted to see my son more than anything, but at what cost? The cost of my life was not my biggest fear, but the loss of my pride and prostituting my body, that was a different matter! I did not want my son to know that his mother sold herself like a common whore. I wanted his respect and love above anything else, not his disgust.

I saw Louis in the great hall many times,

but he did not approach me, but then of course, I had known that he would not. Robert knowing that he had accosted me was something that Louis would wish to remain a secret. I had also stopped walking to the south tower, not wanting to see him until I had decided what to do.

Although I had deliberated other ways and means to free my son, my plans always seemed ridiculous and doomed to fail. It seemed that I could not deny the fact that I needed Louis's help to gain access to my son. This knowledge irritated me so much that it was often in my thoughts, and I became noticeably distracted, to the extent that Robert had started to notice, and he was confused and curious to the reason behind it. He asked me many times what I was thinking, his face studying my response of 'Nothing!' carefully. He was suspicious, and I felt uncomfortable from his scrutiny.

In the end my decision was made for me by Robert's own actions. I had made my way down to the great hall on my way to the stables in anticipation of riding out. I would often ride for hours at a time. I had no chores to do, and unlike most of the vampire women in the manor, I had grown up working on a farm where there was always some chore to do. I had found that I could not get out of the habit of waking at dawn, and within a short while of waking, I would grow bored and restless.

I had explained my dilemma to Robert, and within days, he presented me with a beautiful dappled grey horse. "He will take up your time, my love," Robert had said, an indulgent smile playing on his lips as he witnessed my hugging and petting of the prancing beast, and hearing my words of, "Thank you, oh thank you...His name will be Cesar, it suits him, does it not?" "Yes...yes, I think it does. You can occupy your days by taking him out hunting, ride as long as you like, but remember you must always come back to me!" Although I laughed at his comment, and swore, "Always, Robert, I could never leave you, my love!" I heard the possession and harshness behind his words, and I knew he was issuing me with a warning not to abuse his trust.

I spent hours, almost every day, riding Cesar along the byways, lanes, and woodlands, sometimes riding many miles from Vanike. Of course, there was no need for a companion, I was a vampire, and there was no fear of anyone harming me. If the need should arise, I could kill an attacker quickly and efficiently.

I was surprised to discover that one of my greatest pleasures was to bewitch travelers and feed from them. I tended to favor rich men, mostly because in their arrogance they would rein in beside Cesar and me, and try to exchange pleasantries and charm me. These were the very same men who would have looked down on me when I was a human, and would have probably even decided to try to rape and pillage my body. Ironically, now, because they believed that I was of noble birth, they instead tried to pay court.

It delighted me to feed from them, to place them in the position that previously would have been mine, and to see them powerless and afraid. I would take their blood, and relish the feeling of their strength and vitality flowing through my veins. I stole their wealth, and laughed like a mischievous child as I bewitched them into believing that they had misplaced their purse, and I was in fact simply a daydream. Later as I rode through the small villages on my route, I would openly laugh from throwing their farthings to the poor beings they previously misused. However, I admit with no shame that I gained the most satisfaction from placing their sovereigns in my own coffers.

The truth is that I had grown very rich from the purses of the powerful men I accosted. However, my growing wealth was my secret. I knew that Robert would insist on my handing it over to him if he knew of my wealth, stating that I had no need of money, when he could always give me everything I would ever want or need. I could imagine the frown on his face and his deep voice asking me, *Why did I want my own wealth? Why did I want to flee his love?* I would then, I knew, have no choice but to hand over the gold I had collected, and if I objected - I would alert him to the fact that I was indeed planning to flee from him. Sometimes he would ask me casually if I ever robbed my victims. I would always look shocked. Stating, "You know I would never do that, Robert...I would feel so guilty...no... no, I really could not do that!" His eyes would instantly soften, and often he would lean forward to kiss my nose, whispering, "My sweet; sweet, girl!" I felt guilty for lying to him, but although I loved him, and the truth was that I did, very much, I knew that there were some things I could never tell him. So instead, I rode for miles, collecting my great wealth, and in doing so, I would be able to ensure my son's future.

On the day that finally decided me on the action of following Louis' plan, I had taken the servants' stairs down to the great hall. Since I had realized that Robert would never budge in regards to my having contact with my son, I had stepped up my campaign in waylaying rich strangers and expanding my coffers. The difficulty was that if Robert noticed me preparing to go out riding, he might insist on joining me, and I would forgo my purse of sovereigns for the day; this was not an option, and so I avoided meeting Robert if I could. Robert never used the servants' stairs, and so I had a far lesser chance of running into him.

I made my way stealthily down the stairs, excitement causing adrenaline to race inside me, because I found that I loved the daring of doing something I should not. The servants' stairs exited next to the main entrance to the manor, a large velvet curtain hiding the stairway's location. I always stopped at the curtain, as I did this day, and listened carefully to establish who was on the other side. If I heard voices, I would peek around the curtain, hoping it was no one of significance. If the was the case, I would simply slip out from behind the curtain and make my way to the stables. However, if I recognized the occupants in the hall, I would simply wait for them to leave, and then continue on my way.

On this day, I heard voices, several of them. I cursed under my breath, and pulled the curtain back just enough for me to peek at the occupants of the great hall without giving away my location.

I was shocked and mortified by what I saw! Robert sat in his usual chair by the fireside, and Matilda's head rested on his shoulder. Louis and some of Robert's friends, alongside several of Matilda's women, lounged casually around the happy couple, and my son sat contentedly on Robert's lap.

Henry was almost ten months old, and he was a strong and healthy baby. His little plump face looked up at the sound of Matilda's and Robert's voices, and although he had turned his head and I had lost sight of his face, I heard him chuckle, and I saw his arms reach out to Matilda.

I felt sick. My first glimpse of my beautiful boy, and he was looking towards the woman I hated, looking at her, I was sure, with love and devotion in his eyes. I wanted to run over and grab him from them, wanted to breathe in his baby smell, to run my fingers through his golden curly hair, and to feel his little plump hands in mine.

I hung my head to my chest, trying to

regain control of my emotions, but it seemed that the desire of wanting to watch them engulfed me and once again, I peeped into the life of my son. Matilda had picked up Henry, but she stood with her back towards me. My eyes scanned the others, and it was then that I realised that Louis knew I was there. He smiled in my direction, and then inclined his head, indicating to me that he had seen me.

I turned away from the curtain. I knew his smile meant that he too was certain that I would now take him up on his offer, which of course, now I had seen the scene in the great hall, I would. I walked back up the stairs, my ride forgotten for the day. I would wait a while and then make my way to the south tower, for I knew that Louis would be waiting for me. I also knew that the fate of Robert and me turning from lovers to enemies had been set in the stone of my frosted heart.

Chapter Seven

Just as I had anticipated, when I made way to the south tower Louis was waiting for me in the inner alcove in which he had accosted me the first time he waylaid me. "I see you have made up your mind, mademoiselle," he said, a conceited smile playing around his lips. I felt my hackles immediately rise. Louis' sly demeanor seemed, always, to cause a feeling of revulsion to rise up within me.

I dropped my head, and averted my eyes, not wanting him to see the disgust I felt for him. "Yes, as you know I witnessed the scene in the great hall, but I have no wish to discuss it further..." A sob escaped my throat and my voice died. "I understand, ma petite," he said, but his voice showed no sign of empathy, in fact he sounded like he would burst into laughter at any moment.

Irritation swamped me, and not wanting Louis to witness my weakness I pulled myself up to my full height, and looked Louis square in the eye. "What is your plan?" I asked him abruptly.

"Oh, ma petite...must we talk about such things...we should talk of love, our love."

I was unable to conquer anger flooding my body, my fangs grew in response, and my eyes, I knew, were opaque. "Once I have my son...not before!" I snapped, making it obvious to him how abhorrent the idea of sharing my body with him was to me. A responding anger glowed in Louis' eyes, but he visibly quelled it, and a chilling smile graced his face.

"Of course, ma petite, the garçon is more important, but we will discuss this tomorrow, the day moves on and we will both be missed!" He then bowed, and abruptly turned and walked away.

My mind told me that I should flatter and encourage him, but my heart and body were unable to follow the command. Nevertheless, I decided that the next day that I would try to be more subtle, more persuading, and reassure him that I found him attractive – a task that was not going to be easy.

The following day I met with Louis as planned, but I found it harder than I had anticipated looking into his sly, mean little face and pretending that I found his demeanor pleasant, let alone convey to him that I had softer feelings towards him. However, Louis seemed to appreciate my softer approach, and his smile shone true with no hidden meanings.

"I believe, ma petite, that you have softened towards me?" he exclaimed. I could not agree with him vocally, but simply smiled and inclined my head in a nod of agreement. Nevertheless, my approach seemed to work, and he began to rapidly tell me of his plan for the abduction of my son.

"I have a grand chateau in Aquitaine. I have not told any here, so it will be a safe haven for you and your garçon. I will bewitch the nurse and she will take you up to the child whilst Matilda visits the great hall." Louis paused and grabbed my hand, his voice softening, he then continued, "I will take my leave tonight, but I have bewitched the nurse to take you to the child in three nights' time. Hopefully, Robert will not link my farewell with the disappearance of you both." "But...but how will I know where your chateau is located in Aquitaine?" I asked him anxiously. "Ma petite!" he said, his hand rising to halt my flow of words. "No, no, do you think I would leave you alone? Non, ma petite, I will wait at the inn at the crossroads, you know the one?"

I did know the inn he referred too; I had used it several times for refreshment when out on my rides. "Yes, yes I know the inn," I confirmed. "Good, mon amie, well I will wait for you there. We will then ride to Dover, cross the Channel, and make our way to my chateau. Do you agree with my plan, mademoiselle?"

What could I say? I had no alternative, I needed to agree to his plan if I was to get my son back. "Yes of course I agree. Thank you, Louis." A genuine smile lit his face and he pulled me into his arms, his mouth assaulting mine.   Inwardly I cringed, and I was sure that Louis felt me stiffen in his arms, because as he pulled away, I noticed that his eyes glittered with irritation.

After explaining that the nurse would meet me in the alcove at sunset in three days' time, Louis took his leave. Before leaving, he once more pulled me into his arms, whispering his love for me. I accepted his declaration as graciously as I could and tried to muster a passion that I did not feel, and I knew I never would.

I do not know how I made it through the following days. I rode Cesar like a demon, not bothering to waylay strangers, and although the days passed by in a blur, the nights were a different matter.

The nights had a bittersweet quality for me. I knew that these were the last hours of love I would spend with Robert, and so I put my heart and soul into every action. I clung to him tighter, cherished his touch and kiss more than usual, and poured my soul into sharing my body with him. I loved him, and always would, and I was ensuring that I would remember our time together for all time.

Robert, I was sure, noticed my desperation, and sometimes he would look at me, a puzzled expression on his face. Nevertheless, he never said anything, and seemed to accept my sudden urgency to love him more intensely than usual.

The day of the abduction came quickly. I was nervous and afraid, and very unsure of our future, and so I made my way to the alcove where I was to meet the young nurse. Uncertainty flooded my mind, and several times I attempted to walk away and forget Louis' plan, but no sooner had I turned, than I would turn back to the alcove. I knew that I would not and could not leave my son to the destiny Matilda and Robert had planned for him.

"Hello, are you Gwen?" I swung around to face the small and nervous whisper. Yes, yes I am," I replied, taking in the appearance of the owner of the voice. The girl in front of me was no little more than a child. She was tiny and frail, her skin the colour of a pan of milk. Even her hair looked like the colour was faded, and from her appearance, I knew that she was currently dinner for several vampires. "Follow me, please," she said turning from me, her eyes glazed, giving the impression that her soul had already vacated her body.

I followed her, knowing that I was changing not just my son's destiny, but mine also.

Chapter Eight

I followed the young girl around the narrow stairs that led to the south tower. I was nervous, and constantly looked behind me, afraid that I would suddenly see Matilda's form creeping up the stairs.

The girl never once looked back, Louis had bewitched her well, and she was intent on delivering me to the nursery quickly. When we reached Matilda's bedchamber the girl suddenly turned, she beckoned towards me, and then sped away from me through the room.

As I entered the bedchamber Matilda's familiar scent, a musky smell of cinnamon and some spice that I was unfamiliar with, attacked my senses. I halted, her scent causing me to rapidly gaze around the room to ensure she was not present. Although the room was empty, I felt a threatening presence. However, I could not see or hear anything or anyone, and so I put my hesitation down to the fact that I was shaking from nerves.

I glanced towards the girl who was now beckoning violently me to the small doorway in which she stood. Ignoring the threat I felt in Matilda's bedchamber, I followed the girl into the adjoining room.

On entering the sound of my son's sweet chuckle drifted towards me. I felt my stomach leap with feelings akin to love and anticipation, and I made my way, in a trance-like state, to the corner from which his voice came.

He was the most beautiful baby I had ever seen. His eyes shone bright blue, just like my own, but when he smiled up at me, I saw Tom's sweet face glowing within. The reflection from the fire made his hair shine like burnished copper, his little cheeks were pink and flushed, and when he held up his plump arms for me to hold him, I had such a fierce feeling of love that I thought I would burst from the sheer force of it.

His giggles echoed around the room as I swung him up tightly against my chest, and I laughed aloud at the sound. I brushed his small button nose with my own, and kissed his angelic face repeatedly, breathing in his sweet baby smell as I did so. I wanted to hold him and marvel at his perfection and beauty forever, but I knew that now was not the time for such actions, and with regret, pushed him into the young girl's arms, as I bundled his clothing into a small cloth bag I had found for the purpose.

"Quickly, go through into Matilda's bedchamber," I whispered. Motioning her towards the doorway, "I will follow." I watched her disappear from the doorway and then turned around in a circle, scanning the room for a thick blanket in which to tie Henry to my body and keep him warm. Snatching a blanket from his crib, I made my way through to Matilda's bedchamber.

"*Going somewhere, my love?*" Robert's voice echoed around the spice-scented room. Fear clasped my throat like a vice, and I looked to the girl holding Henry, trying to judge if I would be able to snatch him and escape before Robert could catch me.

"Do not try it, Gwen, *you cannot make it!*" He was right, I knew there was no escape, and so I searched my mind for something, anything, to convince him I had meant no harm. "Don't try what, Robert?" I asked him, trying to inject humor into my voice, "I have no idea what you mean! You've caught me out, I confess, I had hoped to spend an hour with my son; oh I know you're angry, but I only wanted an hour!"

His laughter and his clapping rang out around the room, causing Henry to cry out in fear.

"*Bravo, bravo...my love.*" He walked over so that he was beside the girl and Henry as he spoke.

"But I'm afraid, my love...that a strolling

player you will never be!" I tried to portray that I had no idea what he was talking about, a frown creasing my brow. "Well, Robert, I have no idea what you mean." Like a flash he was beside me, his hand clutched my hair in a painful hold. "Oh really! So why then have you clothes enough for a journey, *my love?* Moreover, why do you shake with fear? And how would I know of a whisper that you intended to steal Henry...pray tell me, *my love?*" I shuddered with fear, for I knew that he would never allow me to live, and that I would never see my son grow.

Pulling myself up to my full height, I looked him in the eye, and said, "So you know? Well I have no excuse, other than I crave my son above anything, I need him...please, oh please understand, Robert." "I do understand, Gwen," He paused, running his finger slowly down my cheek. He then beckoned to the girl, who moved as if in a dream towards him. When she reached him, he gently took Henry from her arms, and then in a move so quick it was barely visible, he thrust his hand into her chest and withdrew her beating heart.

Blood squirted in a wide pumping arc out of the girl's chest, but she still stood for a second, even glanced down at the hole in her bosom, shock apparent on her face, and I watched, stunned, as life left her face and she fell gracefully to the floor. Then Robert knelt and gently placed Henry on the floor beside the girl. I watched in disgust, as he took the girl's heart and handed it to my child, a soft chuckle signaling his approval as Henry hungrily chewed on the warm bloody organ.

Before me was the reason why I needed to get my son away from him, the man I loved was a monster, but I was not, if I was able, going to allow him to turn my son into one. I opened my mouth to speak, but Robert held his hand up to silence me. He still knelt beside Henry, laughing at his antics, but his voice, when he spoke, was for me alone. "Leave, Gwen, leave before I kill you...Leave Vanike, me and your son; I want you gone by sunrise... *otherwise I will kill you!* Never return here, because the day I see you again, Gwen, is the day you will die!"

Chapter Nine

I had already packed all of my clothes and possessions, and had sewn all of my sovereigns into the hems of my dresses, in the days before the attempted abduction of Henry. I therefore had no reason to linger, and although I thought about returning to Robert and begging him to allow me to stay, I was sure this time he would carry out his threat to kill me. The thought of dying meant very little to me, but there was still Henry to consider, and while he was still human, there was still a chance that I could save him.

Tears flooded my eyes as I looked around my bedchamber, and so many memories and images tortured my mind. The night of Henry's birth, Robert, and I sharing our love, memories that would linger with me until the end of my days, memories I would cherish.

I turned away from the images the bedchamber conjured up, and made my way out of the manor. Cesar was ready and waiting for me, so I assumed that word of my attempted abduction of Henry had spread fast. I called out to the stable lad to run to my room and collect my belongings, and told him that I would need a pack pony to transport my luggage. The command was accomplished quickly and quietly, and within a very short time, I had no choice but to ride my horse away from Vanike Manor. I wanted to run to Robert and beg for forgiveness, but I knew it would be a pointless exercise, I had, I guessed, used up all of his mercy quota, and I knew that I would never know his love again.

When I had reached the summit of the incline, I turned to survey what I was to leave behind, and vowed one day to return and save my son, even if it meant my death. I never looked back again; it was time for me to move on.

Part Two

Chapter Ten

I made my way to the inn at the crossroads to meet Louis. I had decided, because the abduction had failed, that I would no longer be leaving with him for France, and I would, instead, find my own way in the world from now on. I had plenty of gold, in truth a vast fortune, and I was more than capable of looking after myself.

On reaching the inn, I jumped off Cesar's back and threw the reins to the stable hand, shouting to him to rub down and feed my horse, for I would be staying the night. I had no sooner crossed the threshold than Louis was by my side, pulling me roughly into his arms. "Louis...Louis!" I said in irritation, shoving him roughly from me. "Please *stop!*" "What is this, ma petite?" he asked, his eyes narrowing in anger. "Why do you treat me so?" "I don't know what you mean, Louis," I said. "I am treating you the same as I always have."

He stepped away from me, his eyes still narrowed, his glance searching up and down my body. "So where is the garçon, ma petite?" he asked. His words hit me hard, reminding me of my failure in rescuing my child, and I fell back against a wooden table, dropping down onto the rough bench that ran alongside it. "Robert was there, and, and... my son...my son, he is lost to me!"

Louis was concerned by my words, his face showed a worried frown, and his words were soft and persuading. "Come, ma petite, we will discuss this in private with a glass of wine." His hand reached out to mine, and pulling me up from the bench, he said, "Come, ma petite."

With his hand still gripping mine tightly, I followed him into a small room at the back of the inn. Glancing towards the rough wood table in the corner of the small room, I noticed that there was wine and two goblets sitting on the table. Louis had, it seemed, already acquired the small room and had ordered wine for our use. I sat heavily on one of the wooden chairs provided, and took a huge gulp of wine.

"What am I to do?" I asked Louis as I looked up into his face. I noticed that his eyes glittered, and that he watched me intently as I drunk. "I do not know, ma petite." He shrugged. I felt instant irritation by his lack of concern, and decided that it was time to tell him that I would be making my own way and not joining him in France.

"I have decided to stay in England," I said, rising to my feet, but something was wrong. My head swayed, and I felt faint, a feeling that I had not felt since becoming a vampire. Falling back into the chair, I gripped the table with one hand and gripped my head with my other. "Are you ill, ma petite?" Louis asked, bending over me.

"No... No I am fine," I said, waving away his face, which was very close to my own, but the truth was I did not feel fine, I felt ill. My body felt limp and lifeless, my head was pounding and spinning and my hands shook.

Louis walked over to the small fire that provided the room with warmth, his back to me. "What is wrong with me?" I whispered and took another few mouthfuls of wine, hoping it would stop my shaking. It was only then that I realised that it tasted strange and was bitter with the undertone of metallic but foul-tasting blood. No sooner had I drunk the wine than I felt worse, and found it difficult to stay seated. My body felt weaker and could feel my strength ebbing away.

"Oh dear, ma petite, it looks like you have been poisoned!" I turned my head, with difficulty, towards him. He had moved away from the fire, and was once more standing beside me. I opened my mouth to question him, but was unable to speak, my mouth and body felt rigid and I had lost control of my limbs. I slid down on to the cold dirt floor, my body crumpled and useless.

Louis knelt down beside me with his face close to mine, a manic smile on his lips, and his eyes shining with malice. "Ah, mon amie...mon amie...you should be careful who you trust. It was me, ma petite, I sent message to Robert that you were going to snatch the garçon."

I wanted to scream at him, to claw his eyes out, and thrust a stake through his heart! He had betrayed me, but above this, he had lost me my son. A deep chuckle rumbled in his chest. "Ah, my sweet, your eyes are shining...you wish to kill me, oui? I love you, man petite...but it is in vain, is it not?" He laughed, but it sounded like a crazy manic scream. "You see, I could not take your garçon, ma petite, Robert would have tracked us down, he would have killed us...but I wanted you, mon amie...and so I have you!"

He ran his finger down my cheek. Disgust raged through my body, but I could not voice it or act upon it, and so I was helpless and trapped with a cruel and crazy abductor. "You will come to love me, ma petite...but it will take time, my sweet... and luckily we have all the time in the world."

Louis rose from the floor and walked towards the table, but I was unable to see what he was doing because paralysis had taken over my body. When he returned and once more knelt down beside me, he held the goblet of wine to my mouth, lifted my head, and poured the foul-tasting liquid down my throat.

"You did not know of this weakness, did you, mon amie? Ah, no matter, I will explain, you see...we cannot drink blood from a dead body. It renders us helpless, as you now know, it poisons us...you will sleep, ma petite...but never die...sometimes wake, but be hardly able to move...and you will be mine, always."

My mind grew fuzzy and my eyes grew dim. I heard Louis chuckle, and I knew that I was trapped in a hell of his making. The last thing I felt as I drifted into sleep was a single tear make its way slowly down my frozen cheek.

Chapter Eleven

I awoke feeling disorientated, my mouth was dry, and I could barely swallow. It took a moment for me to recall what had happened. A queasy feeling attacked me, I rolled from side to side, and I quickly realised that we were traveling across the English Channel on our way to France. This realization brought vomit to my throat, and it tasted of the stale blood and wine Louis had forced me to drink.

I tried to move, but I was unable to, due to the effects of the blood, and even if this was not the case, I was confined, crushed into a wooden chest. Suddenly, the lid of the chest opened, and Louis' face danced in front of me.

"You must drink, ma petite," he said, holding the stale wine to my lips. I moved my head from side to side in an attempt to evade the foul invasion that he was once again going to force my body to accept, but it was to no avail, and I heard him giggle as the wine filled my mouth and flowed down my throat. The sound of which echoed in my dazed mind as I once again fell into a tortuous coma.

Many times I awoke to the feel of rocking, and the sound of crashing waves, but every time Louis swooped down upon me, ready and waiting to fill my body with the stale blood that would keep me his prisoner. At times, just before Louis arrived, I would feel rats scurrying over my body. I even felt their teeth sink into my flesh, their squeals of angered possession pounding my crazed mind.

Sometimes I thought I heard a baby cry, and sometimes I thought I heard Robert's voice. My spirits at these times rose high, for I believed in my hallucinated state that he had arrived to rescue me from Louis, my son with him, and we would live happily together forever. I would then see Louis' face floating above me, my dream would turn into a nightmare, my laughter into screams, and once again, I would fall into the dark abyss that was Louis' prison.

After a while, I awoke to the sound of horses' hooves pounding against dry earth and the shuddering feeling of a rickety carriage. Complete darkness surrounded me, I tried to bang on the lid of the chest, even dreamed of escape, but I was still incapacitated, still barely able to move. Instead, I let my mind wander, I remembered the farm where I grew up, and my mother's soft face offering me a tankard of sweet warm milk. In my confused state, I reached out to her, and although her fingers reached for me, we never quite joined hands. Bittersweet tears of sorrow engulfed me, and silent cries of grief, caused by my loss, echoed deep within my soul. .

My memories swamped me. Sometimes, I would find myself making love to Tom in a sweet meadow, his face so loving and beautiful, but then his features would be replaced by Robert's, and excitement would send my body into a passionate frenzy. In the deepest throes of my lust, I would look up, and glimpse Tom hanging from a tree, his entrails ripped from his body, and I would pray, half crazed, for forgiveness, to a God that would no longer welcome me into His fold.

Cramps attacked my gut and I returned to the day I gave birth to Henry. I held my stomach, I felt the huge swelling of my pregnancy, and I cried with joy. I would be able to save my son; I would not give him to Robert. I laughed hysterically! Suddenly Matilda's face hovered above me, but she held something in her hand, as I looked closer I realised it was a knife, and I knew she was going to cut my son from me again. I started to plead with her in high-pitched screams, but her voice squealed much higher than mine as she yelled, "Ma petite...Ma petite!" Then her face changed, and the features in front of me changed into those of Louis, and the knife turned into a goblet of wine. I choke and cough in protest as the wine floods my throat and pours over my face, I smell the stench of stale blood, and then I feel my body once more descend into a floating numbness. Louis' fingers caress my face with soft strokes, his voice uttering loving words of endearment, and I am sinking into the depths of insanity. The approaching darkness becomes a blessed relief, and I sink gratefully into its arms, hoping to escape Louis and the torture of my mind.

My reality is now a perpetual nightmare, sometimes I see Louis' face, and at others, different faces from my past. They terrified me by their lust for revenge and their frenzied cries. I felt their hands claw at my face, their teeth ravage me in searing rage, and I prayed for help that I knew would never come. I wanted to escape the evil terror I was experiencing, but my mind held me prisoner, and deep down I knew I was encased, for all time, in the world of horror that Louis had created for me.

Before long I noticed that my circumstances had changed. I no longer swayed with the rocking of waves, or heard the pounding of horses' hooves, and through my muddled mind, I started to realise that I had finally arrived at my destination.

"Ma petite...It is time for you to wake, mon amie."

Louis' voice penetrated my muddled thoughts, and although my eyelids were heavy, I managed to force them open so that I could survey my surroundings.

"Where...where am I?" I asked, my voice no more than a raspy whisper. "We are home, mon amie...look around you, ma petite."

I raised my aching head with difficulty to look around the room. The first thing I noticed was that my arms and legs were bound to the four corners of a bed. I still could not feel my limbs, they were numb, and unless I had looked, I would not have known that I was shackled like an animal to the bed.

The bed was unlike any I had seen and was huge. Elegant curtains of beautiful deep red blood-colored silks and satins, draped all around me in a haze of adornment. It was a bed fit for a queen in its elegance and grandiose style. I surveyed the rest of the room, and like the bed, the decoration, of red, gold, beautiful furniture and rich fabrics, were more befitting a person of high status - it was very French-looking, and extremely breathtaking to survey.

I noticed my luggage stacked against the wall, and was relieved that at least my personal possessions and my coffers had followed me untouched. Louis followed my gaze and his voice floated towards me.

"Ma petite...your possessions are all there, I am not unreasonable, and wish for you to feel...what is the word...oui...comfortable." A raspy laugh escaped my throat, but I felt no joy, and it was a sarcastic laugh of contempt. "Why, Louis...why should I be comfortable when you keep me bound and poisoned, a prisoner...*A PRISONER, LOUIS*?"

Louis started to pace in front of me, irritation causing his movements to look jerky and awkward. "I have no choice, mon amie, you will be my prisoner until you decide not to be...and then you will be my love, my sweet...but until then...I am sorry, ma petite, but you will be...as you say, my prisoner and my lover!"

His words confused me, I could not be his lover, I was his prisoner; how then, could I be his lover? Then his meaning vibrated inside my head with resounding clarification. "You intend to rape me, Louis?" my voice escaped my throat in a croaky whisper, sounding weak and defeated, even to my own ears.

"Non! Non, my love...you wish this, tell me you wish this!"

He moved to my side, his face soft and loving, waiting for my consent. "No, Louis," I whispered, "Never, *NEVER!*" His face contorted with anger, and his hands reached out to the bodice of my gown. The sound of the material ripping filled the room. My body was numb, but I imagined the rush of cold sweeping my uncovered skin. I tried to lift my head to look at my now exposed and vulnerable body, but I no longer had the strength of will to witness his pillage of me. I closed my eyes as Louis climbed on top of me.

Louis' sighs filled the room. Hour after hour, I heard him take pleasure from my vulnerability. When the numbness of the poisoned wine wore off, I felt his grasping fingers delve into the soft and once yielding parts of me. Parts that should have felt pleasure from a man's touch, and not petrified disgust at an animal's betrayal. I was bound by pain, as he bit into that softness, but he sucked none of the tainted blood from me, and so I remained motionless and weak. I felt his manhood, hard and stabbing, enter me, but there was no joy, and I felt his lust tear my skin in its relentless pursuit of pleasure.

When my body started to jerk and move angrily from the horror of his rape. Louis calmly slid off me. "I think that is enough for today," he said, his voice breathless and triumphant.

He moved away from me, but I did not watch him leave. My eyes shut tightly, and my shame curdled like rotten milk inside of me. Louis once more returned to my side, lifted my head, and poured the tainted wine into my mouth, but this time he didn't have need to force me. I drank willingly, knowing that it would help me escape the hell of Louis's torture, and when the now familiar feeling of the poison overtook my body, I embraced it like an old friend.

Chapter Twelve

Day and night Louis subjected me to his lust and anger. Time had no meaning for me, and I lived in a perpetual loop that consisted of torture, horror, and strangely enough - love. I escaped into a world of fantasy, joined by the people that I had loved and lost. Sometimes the world I entered would turn ugly, and I would face the horror of watching Tom hang, or his mother Martha's body, grotesquely laid out on her kitchen table. Although mostly, my dreams, embraced me with love and hope, and my former loved ones held me gently in the aftermath of Louis' frequent battering of my body and soul.

Every time Louis would ask me if I would come to him willingly, and many times I was tempted to submit to his will, but I could not, as long as I had my protectors in my dreams, I knew I would survive.

Sometimes Louis would inform me of what was going on in the world. I would listen to his irritating voice relaying events that I could not participate in and so I would will myself to escape into the fantasy world I had created.

Louis informed me when King Henry died, and when his nine-year-old son, Edward, became King of England. My thoughts drifted away and I conjured up the young girl that I had met, the girl who had been Henry's queen at the time. She was such a young girl to be married to an old tyrant like Henry. Poor Catherine Howard, so sweet, beautiful, and full of life, and Henry, the selfish, greedy king who had condemned her to death, and had cut short the sound of her musical laughter. Thereafter, Catherine materialized in my dreams and joined the people that held me when I laughed and cried. He told me when Edwards's sister Mary became queen, and how she had gained the alias 'Bloody Mary' because of her lust for condemning her subjects to death. I listened to his tales of murder and pillage for a while, and then once more I would conjure my protectors to shield me from the violence of his need.

Then one day, I know not the day of the week or the date, Louis came to me and talked to me of Elizabeth, the new queen of England. I was somewhat more alert than usual on this day, because I answered him, "But how is it possible that she is Queen, Louis...she is but a child." "Mon amie...but the mademoiselle is no longer a child... she is a beautiful woman, or so I am told." His laughter surrounded me, and his voice was musical and light. It occurred to me, quite suddenly, that I had been Louis' prisoner much longer than I had realised.

I tried to lift my head, but fell back on the bed feeling faint. "Louis," I said in a tormented whisper, "Louis, what year is it?" Louis' face moved close to mine, his face a mask of kindness. "It is 1558, mon amie...you have slept for a long time...are you ready to wake?"

The year was 1558, but that was impossible! If the year was indeed 1558, then I had been Louis' captive for sixteen years. I heard Louis' words echo inside my muddled brain; *Are you ready to wake?* My thoughts returned to my son, my son who had grown into adulthood, as I lay captive, Henry, my beautiful son, who would become a vampire on his eighteenth birthday. Suddenly, I knew that I needed to submit to Louis and find a way to leave the prison he had created for me.

"Yes, Louis, I am ready to become yours." I saw a frown flitter across his brow. "Why now... mademoiselle?" he asked, his eyes watching mine intently. "Because I am ready, Louis, I want to hold you...I want...no, need...I need your love."

I must have convinced him I was sincere, for his face blazed with triumph. His joy was so great that he ripped away the chains that held me to the bed with his bare hands. He held my body in a soft and gentle embrace, and gently lowering my head so that it was positioned close to his neck, he whispered, "Drink, ma petite...drink, my love."

I drank from him, and instantly I felt my strength return, my body tingled as it awoke, and I felt my senses soar. "Mon amie...steady...steady," Louis said as he pulled away from my grasp. I let him pull away, for it was my intention to gain his trust, and I wanted him to believe for the moment that I loved him. "I thought you would wish to kill me, mon amie." Louis said, his hold on my body still tight, I giggled, and said, "Oh no, Louis...I need you...I need you, my darling..." I did need Louis, until the time was right, then I would kill him.

Chapter Thirteen

Slowly, very slowly, I regained my strength. I had been captive in my prison of the mind for sixteen years and although I was a vampire and my body healed quickly, I was still very thin, and at times weak. I also found it difficult to shake my protectors, my mind continued to search for them, and I would see them day and night. They appeared in the shadows when I needed them, and often I would see their faces peeking behind the curtain of the bed at the moment Louis arrived in my bedchamber to ravage my body.

I had ascertained that Queen Elizabeth had come to the throne in the middle of November. We were now at the end of

December and I had just under a year to stop my son becoming a vampire. I needed to get well quickly, and return to England with all haste. I was aware that time was running out, and that my son needed me now more than ever.

Louis came to trust me very quickly. I believe that in his arrogance he believed that my imprisonment had broken my spirit, and that I was afraid of him. Of course, I let him believe his theory, and would often make a play of cowering slightly when he approached me. I became adept at deferring to him on his opinions and making those opinions my own, ensuring that his ego grew, and that his defenses lowered with the idea of his own self-worth.

It was approaching February when I decided that Louis trusted me enough to allow me to carry out my plan without complication. I was fit and strong again, although I pretended to be otherwise, and more importantly, time was moving on, I needed to make my way to England soon.

I had arranged for us to dine in our private dining room. The chateau had very many grand rooms, and they all were filled with treasures and wealth, but I needed privacy for my plan to work.

Louis, like many vampires, adored a live feast. I abhorred the thought of dining decadently on a live human, making it a pleasure and entertainment. Maybe I was a hypocrite, for after all, I drank freely from the servants in the chateau, but somehow it seemed wrong to make a spectacle of our deprivation, and more importantly our lack of respect for human life. Tonight, however, I would give Louis what he loved, for it was vital to my plan.

I had bewitched one of the prettiest serving girls and led her into our small private room already naked. I could tell from the way his eyes lit up, that Louis felt excitement by this change in me, and he was pleased that I offered to him that what he adored, even though it was distasteful to me. "Ma petite...but you loathe the live feast...is that not so?" he asked, rising slightly from his chair as I helped the young woman arrange herself artfully on the table.

Walking around the table, I pushed Louis gently back into his seat, and leaning forward I whispered in his ear, "Shh, my darling...this is my gift to you, my love...sit back and enjoy." "Ah, ma petite..." he whispered, his voice deep and passionate, he relaxed back in his chair, expectancy shining from deep within his eyes.

Once more, I returned to the woman and taking her soft white hand, I gently turned it over. I picked up a small silver dagger I had already placed on the table, and drew it swiftly across her wrist. I licked at the blood that squirted from her, and then placed a silver goblet, which I had already prepared, under her wrist to catch the blood and from which I would serve Louis.

I swirled the blood in the goblet as I made my way with swinging hips towards him. Lust shone out from his glowing face, and he was barely able to contain himself in his seat, his want of the gift I was offering him was so great. Running my tongue around the rim of the goblet before I lowered it to his waiting mouth, I said, "This will prove to you my love, my sweet."

His eyes never left mine as he took the goblet from my hand and gulped the contents down. I waited and I watched, and then I had the greatest reward as his hand started to shake, and his eyes glazed over. "What have you done, ma petite?" he asked, his voice barely a whisper.

I walked behind him, placed my mouth next to his ear and whispered, "Oh Louis, Louis, did you think I would forgive you after what you did to me? No, Louis...Oh no, no, no, you have, my love, ingested the foul decaying blood of a rat that's been dead and rotting for just over two days."

I giggled as Louis' answering gurgle reached me, I watched with glee as he slid, defenseless, to the floor. I pushed his chair back and out of the way, so that I had a clearer view of him. I then stepped over his pathetic body, and kneeling down beside him I said, "The difference is,

Louis, I really do not want to take you as my prisoner, I do not want you in my life...and that leaves me with a dilemma! You see, my love, if I leave you alive I have no doubt that you will try and find me, and either take me once more as your prisoner or maybe even kill me. I do not want that, Louis, and so I have no alternative."

Reaching behind me, I took hold of the chair Louis had sat upon, and with slow intent snapped off one of the legs. His eyes followed my actions, and he knew, I had no doubt, what I was intent on doing. "I'm sorry, Louis, but you stole my life, and my body, but more importantly you stole time... time I could have spent with my son...Goodbye, Louis!"

I thrust the improvised dagger deep into his heart and watched his body crumple. His skin faded to grey, his eyes became void of life, and his body became still.

I watched him for a moment, I felt no regret, but I did feel anger. I was angry at the fact that Louis had made the choices that he did, and in doing so, his actions had forced me into taking his life. I would have preferred not to have taken such action, but I really had no choice in the matter. However, having no choice did not make me any less a murderer, and I felt sickened by the fact.

Rising up from his side, I made my way wearily to my bedchamber. I had already packed my possessions, but I wished to take some of the treasures of the house. I rang my bell and asked the girl who answered my call, to bid Henri, Louis' manservant, to attend me.

Henri was a very powerful man, he was tall and strong, and his face shone with evil and malice. When I first made my plan on how to escape Louis, my first thought was: how I would be able to win Henri's support, for I did not wish to receive his wrath.

"You wished to see me, mademoiselle?" he asked from the door of my bedchamber, his body taking up the whole of the doorframe. I smiled towards him, but he did not return the courtesy, and so I simply beckoned him into my room.

"Henri, are you a rich man?" I asked him and saw a look of bewilderment cross his face. "Non... as you know, mademoiselle... I am not," he stated abruptly. "No, I thought not, well, Henri...how would you like to benefit from the riches of the chateau while I'm away on my travels? I will leave the lands to your care, and you may keep all of the profit that you make. The only thing I will ask in return is that you keep, and pay, just a couple of servants in service, who will be engaged to look after the chateau whilst I'm away." Once more a look of confusion chased along his features, but now I saw hope and greed flit across his face also, and I was certain that my plan would succeed. "I have killed your master, Henri..." I waited for him to move towards me in anger, but he did not, although his hand did reach towards the sheathed dagger that was in his belt.

"I will be leaving for a while, but all I will be taking with me is a cart and horses, a few servants, my jewels and some of the fine cloths that hang around my bed. If you will allow this, then you shall profit from the lands, and on my return you will still hold the rights to this land...you will, of course, become a rich man."

Henri bent his head towards his chest. I was at first unsure of what his answer would be, and I started to doubt my earlier thoughts of success, but after a few moments, he lifted his head, and looked into my eyes, his shone with triumph, and I knew that success was mine.

The atmosphere in the chateau changed over the next few days, instead of dark and broody it became light and happy. Servants no longer crept around hiding in shadows, nor were they afraid to speak in my presence or look into my face. Instead of the wrath of these people, as I was expecting, they were instead grateful that I had freed them from Louis. I had discovered that his hold over the chateau had lasted for just over one hundred years, and that he had ruled the servants with violence and terror.

Even Henri, who had always previously seemed to be gruff and irritated, had changed radically. He now walked the corridors of the chateau, a smile ready on his face, and a merry whistle chirping from his lips.

He had changed so much, that he had even told me of his plans for the land surrounding the chateau. He had decided to grow grapevines and he had asked many of the families already living in and around the chateau to join him. Apparently, many of them had agreed that they all would work together and profit from the gift I had bestowed on them.

Any guilt that I felt for Louis' death evaporated in the face of the happiness of these people. I had taken their lives back from the tyrant who stole them, and in doing so, I had given them a reason to live and thrive.

Life for me changed also. Now that I was no longer Louis' prisoner, I started to ride around the countryside surrounding the chateau - the area was stunning! The chateau was nestled in the shade of rolling spring green hills, very much like the English countryside, but more serene. The air was warm, and although it was wintertime, it was warm enough to ride along the lanes without the need of heavy furs and capes.

Several times, I rode into Bordeaux, the closest town to the chateau, and soon enough I became spellbound by the beauty and vibrancy of the town. The people were all cheerful as they strolled through the cobbled lanes selling their wares, laughing and joking with each other, and me also, as I passed them by. Unlike the peasants' buildings in English villages and towns, here people grew wild roses around their doorways, the smell of which was intoxicating. They seemed to love life, their homes, and more importantly each other – I adored it.

I purchased flowers, fruit, bread and cheese, I had no need of any of the goods, but I loved talking to the sellers, and for the first time in a very long time, I felt I was alive and above all else - normal.

Alas, of course, it could not last, and all too quickly it was time for me to begin the long journey to England. I chose five servants to accompany me; two girls, one being a young girl called Marie, and the other was the naked girl from Louis' live feast. I had healed the slash across her wrist with my own blood, and had insisted on tending to her needs myself. In doing so, I had grown attached to her, and she too felt the bond we shared, for she followed me constantly – her name was Jeanne. The men I chose to accompany us were: two young stable hands, both of whom were named Jean, and a third, who was a strong and ruthless man of arms known as Andre.

It was with regret that I bade farewell to my new friends at the chateau. I left with my troop of servants, jewels, and the treasures and cloths I had taken from the chateau hidden in the cart that followed behind me. I vowed I would soon return, but I would not be alone, for if I was to have my way, then I would be returning, accompanied by my son.

It took several weeks to cross the countryside of France and reach the port of Calais. Of course, when I had made my way across the landscape the last time, I had had no view of the places that I passed. Now the glorious landscapes that we rode through mesmerized me. France was a charming country, and although I knew that England would always be my first love, I had started to believe that I would be able to make this country my home on my return.

Likewise, my journey back across the English Channel was somewhat different. Instead of being barricaded into the bowels of hell, below decks, where rats gnawed on my sick and decaying body, I walked along the deck of the ship, my hair blowing in the wind, the smell of the ocean breeze tantalizingly sweet on the air. It was, I believe, on that return journey that my lifelong love of the ocean began.

At night I would creep up to the deck, and holding on to the wood at the stern of the ship, I would inhale the freedom that I knew lurked beneath the rolling waves.

One night, a storm swirled in the depths below, and the ship rolled high and low. I held so tight to the wood that my nails dug in, but I laughed, and I felt as if I was at one with the elements, I was part of the raging wildness, and I belonged.

Before very long, as with all things, my journey ended. The ship I traveled upon glided past the magnificent white cliffs of Dover. Although the vessel was a little battered and limping from the storm, it was still strong, and more than ready to conquer the beast on its return journey.

I too was slightly battered and weather-worn, but I was stronger than ever before, and finally, I had returned home to free my son.

Part Three

Chapter Fourteen

I returned to grounds of Vanike Manor in the April of 1559. The sun shone lightly through the trees, casting sparkling light and contrasting dark shadows on the beautiful English landscape. My heart constricted with love for my homeland.

Of course, it would be impossible for me to enter the manor, so instead I stayed on the outskirts of the estate, hoping for a glimpse of Henry, but dreading that I would see Robert. Robert's warning still echoed with clarity inside my head, and I knew that he would fulfill his promise to kill me. If he so much as glimpsed me through the trees, he would know why I had returned, and would slay me without a second thought.

I prowled the grounds of the manor for two weeks, watching and waiting for a glimpse of the man my son had become. I wondered several times if I would recognise him, and whether maybe I had already passed him on the track leading to

99

the crossroads inn where I stayed at night. I would then shake the thought from my mind, knowing that I would know my son, who as a baby looked so much like Tom.

On my return to the inn, the innkeeper would always sidle up, his smile and manner as sly as a fox. "Food, my lady?" he would ask in a slimy voice, his shining eyes downcast, and his manner subservient.

Every night my small party and I partook of food in the back room, the room that had seen the start of Louis' imprisonment of my body and soul - and I hated the place! Just as I hated the sly innkeeper, but it was a means to an end and so, I knew, it was a nuisance that must be endured.

"Yes, bring food, and your best wine, the day grows cold and I wish to be warmed." Of course, I would not be eating the food, I feed from my servants, and so I wished them to be well fed and content. I was also partial to the warmed wine the innkeeper offered, it acted as a substitute for blood from time to time.

I stood by the roaring fire, my mind as always on Henry and his whereabouts. The innkeeper talked, as he usually did, whilst laying the table with pies and hunks of meat for my party. I always ignored him, he was obnoxious and irritating, and I found his words boring and repetitive.

"Be a great day for the master it be, the young master, well he be a favorite of our Queen Bess, and she be staying at the manor tonight...I offered my services, but the master said, thank you kindly Jack but we be fine."

Instantly I was by his side. "What did you say?" I croaked. "Be a great day..." I stopped his flow of words with the wave of my hand. "Yes, yes, I heard that part...but who pray is the master and young master, mayhap that I know them?"

It was the first time that I had engaged the innkeeper in normal conversation. He held his head slightly higher; his sly, evil eyes were, for once, looking towards my own.

"The master he be the Lord Robert Vanike, and the young master be his son Master Henry."

I stood staring at the innkeeper, thoughts circling my mind. Of course! This was the reason I had not glimpsed them, they had been at the queen's court. "You be knowing of 'em, my lady?" the innkeeper asked. Turning away from his sly knowing gaze I said, "No, no, I don't believe I do...what a pity, they sound very exciting...still my party is waiting for food...so get on with it, man."

After mumbling a response, the innkeeper continued with the task of feeding my party. I stared into the fire, my mind racing, how stupid of me not to realise that Robert would present Henry at court. He had been good friends with King Henry, and so it would make sense that he would wish to be good friends with his heirs and the present monarch.

I gazed into the flames of the fire, trying to decide what would be my next move. Turning towards my party, I watched the innkeeper make his way around the table, and just before he left the room I said, "Innkeeper, we will be leaving tomorrow...ask the stable hand to have my cart ready at cock crow."

The innkeeper looked irritated at my sudden request, but did not remark on it, and bowing his head said, "As you wish, my lady."

It was as I wished, the innkeeper watched too intently, saw too much, and tried to gain too much knowledge. Besides, I was in no doubt that the royal party would be returning to Whitehall soon, and if Henry actually was the favorite of Queen Bess, then Henry would surely follow.

Chapter Fifteen

We rode into London a few days later. I had realized that I would need to bewitch my way into Whitehall, if I was to discover the secrets of Henry's life. I had decided that I would dress as a serving wench, and gain information from whoever or wherever I could gain it. Because I was going to be wearing a disguise as a serving wench, I had found my party an inn about half a mile from Whitehall. I did not want anyone recognizing me coming and going from the royal palace.

I was impatient to find out as much as I could about my son and the life he had led up until that moment, and so I started out towards the palace, shortly after I arrived. I dressed myself in one of my Jeanne's dresses and swiftly made my way to the palace.

It seems that sometimes the fates are for, or against us. However, on this day the fates were on my side, for no sooner had I made my way through the gates of the palace than I heard a young girl whispering about Master Vanike.

"Do you work for Master Vanike?" I asked her, looking deep into her eyes, willing her to talk to me. "Lord no...I works for his betrothed I do...they be getting married, ya see." "And who is his betrothed?" I asked. My eyes were glued to hers, willing her under my spell, because it was vital that I discover all she knew.

The girl paused. I could see she was trying to place me in the palace, trying to recognise me amongst the hundreds that worked there. "What is your name?" I said softly. "I be Anne...and you be?" I smiled at her, and replied, "My name is Jenny. Do you not remember me, Anne? We once worked together for a while in the laundry." A smile lit Anne's face, I had convinced her that she knew of a memory that did not exist, but she could place me now, and therefore trust me.

"Why a course you be Jenny, I near forgot ya, I did...I be working for Lady Jane Simpson, Jenny...she be marrying the young master a few weeks hence."

I was a little startled by Anne's news. Why would Henry marry just a few months before he was to become a vampire? I then noticed that Anne had turned from me and had started to move on.

"Stop, Anne..." I shouted as I caught up to her, holding onto her arm as I turned her towards me. "Do you have any secrets you need to tell me about the lady Jane?" Anne's brow creased in uncertainty, and then looking around her to make sure no one else heard, she said, "Shh, Jenny, the like of us cannot be discussing them, but I do have a secret...she be with child, the lady Jane, that is...she be with child."

Henry had begot his heir before he lost the ability, he would have a child of his own blood, but still become a vampire. I knew without doubt that this was Robert's idea, and anger rushed through my veins. He was using my blood to start a vampire dynasty, a dynasty of murderous beings!

Once more Anne had moved away from me, this time I ran after her and said, "Anne, I think I will attend the lady Jane with you, lead me to her." "But, Jenny, I be getting in trouble...I be." I raised my hand to stop her chatter, and said, "She will be happy to see me, Jenny, it's been a long time, and she's missed me." A smile fluttered across Anne's face. "Of course, Jenny, sure I had forgot that you be friends...Well follow me, Jenny...Follow me."

I followed Anne through the cold corridors of Whitehall. My emotions were all tangled and confused. On the one hand I was happy at the thought that I would soon see a child of my blood enter the world, on the other, I was angry that this child was begot simply to become another monster. Now, more than ever, it was vital that I try to stop Henry changing into a vampire.

Before long, I followed Anne into a large and richly decorated bedchamber. A young girl stood up from a warm chair from beside the fire. She was an angelic vision, a glorious creature of pale golden beauty. Ethereal and fragile, she would never survive in the world of vampires.

"Who is this, Anne?" she asked, her voice, like her body, soft and gentle. Before Anne could answer, I stepped forward. "I am Jenny, Lady Jane. I have waited on you before...I am your friend, my lady..."

Jane walked towards me, her small body wrapped itself into my arms, and in an instant I heard the twin heartbeat of a girl and a boy inside her small childlike body. "Where have you been, Jenny?" She asked me in a quivering voice, "I am afraid...so afraid." "Shh, for I am here now...I am here," I said, as I gently stroked her back.

Chapter Sixteen

Jane fell under my spell with such ease, and she would go along with my slightest suggestion. She confirmed falsely that I had helped look after her when she was a small child, but I had disappeared from her home; when her parents were brutally murdered during the reign of Bloody Mary. She invented memories, memories that I had no part in planting into her fragile mind. She seemed to be so in need of love, so unsure of her worth, and she became dependent on me in just a few days. It was not difficult for me to see how Robert and Henry were able to manipulate this poor vulnerable girl.

I shared her time, made her laugh, and waited beside her patiently for her betrothed to return. She told me that she had known Henry from childhood, from before her parents died. She had always loved him, and she believed he loved her also, but like all men favored by the queen, he must pretend that his eyes were for the beguiling monarch alone. I listened carefully, catching glimpses of the years in Henry's life that I had missed.

I found myself wishing, more than ever, that I could have watched him grow. Nevertheless, I was thrilled that I had found a small way back to those years, via Jane.

The day I met my adult son, was no different from any other day in the palace. I sat, as I usually did now, with Jane beside the fire, in fact, Jane rarely moved from the fireside, and complained that she was constantly cold. We were discussing the wedding plans, Jane talked wistfully of Henry, and how handsome he would be on the day that they finally became one. We were both startled as a gust of wind shook the bedchamber, slamming a door and whistling a howl. Suddenly the door opened and in that fleeting moment my son appeared, pulled Jane from her chair, and swung her around in excitement.

On first seeing him, I wondered how I had ever believed that I might not recognise his face. He looked so much like Tom. His shoulders were strong and wide, his frame tall, and his hair shone like burnished sunlight. I held my breath, I so wanted to run into his arms, to tell him how much I loved and missed him, and to hold this grown man against my chest, and coddle him forever.

"And who is this fair maid, Jane?" I looked up into his eyes, and saw my own staring back at me. For although the rest of him resembled Tom, his eyes were mine. The same thought must have crossed his mind because I saw a frown twist his brow. "This is Jenny...Oh, Henry, you must remember Jenny. She used to play with us when we were tiny. Her mother was Anna, my nurse..."

Henry had turned towards Jane; he now turned back towards me. His eyes narrowed, and I could tell that he was not convinced at all, by the nurse story. My son, I could tell, was far from stupid, and he believed that something was amiss - he just did not know what.

"I am afraid I do not remember you, Jenny...but a friend of Jane's is a friend of mine...and it is a pleasure to meet you." I curtsied, bowing my head low. I knew that I dare not look up into his eyes again, he was suspicious enough, and I had no wish to enhance those suspicions.

I walked to the back of the bedchamber, making pretence of packing away linens and materials. I wanted to give them privacy, but I also wanted to hear what they discussed.

"I have missed you so, Henry," I heard Jane gasp as Henry pulled her into his grasp and kissed her passionately. "As I have you, my sweet...as I have you." "Must you tend the Queen, can we not just run away...I hate it that she takes you from me."

I heard the plea in Jane's voice and winced, willing her to be stronger, weakness would only anger a man such as my son had become.

"Jane, we have discussed this...it is what must be, we must pay court to the Queen...My father discussed this with you..." "Oh, your father..." Jane said, turning away from him, "and is he at court, may I ask?" "No... he is still at Vanike...he is...indisposed at the moment...We will travel back to Vanike soon, my love...we must marry before the child becomes apparent. The Queen, of course, will be present." I heard the irritation in Henry's voice; it was obvious that he did not enjoy having to explaining himself. "Is that is all you care about? The child I carry, the Queen, and your father! *WHAT ABOUT ME HENRY...WHAT ABOUT ME?"*

"Be quiet, you fool! Do you want the whole court to hear our private affairs?"

The previous irritation I had heard in his voice had now turned to anger. I heard Jane sob, and heard the heavy footfall of Henry walking towards the door. I turned as he approached.

"You..." he barked, "You are her woman, are you not?" I nodded, unsure of what to say or do. "Good, well tend to her, will you!" He then walked through the door, slamming it shut as he did so.

Chapter Seventeen

I felt like I was afloat in a hazy cloud of happiness in the days that followed, and I cherished every moment that I spent close to my son. For the first time since Robert had stepped into my life, I felt content and complete. Henry was a fine man; he was strong but kind, with just a hint of cruelty hidden just beneath the surface. Of course, that was only to be expected; he was, after all is said and done, given human hearts to juggle as a child.

I loved to watch him deal with Jane; she was, I should point out, of a very nervous disposition. Henry, however, was so patient with her, and although I was certain that Robert had ordered him to marry Jane, his concern for her wellbeing never seemed to be false or an act. I was proud of the man my son had become.

However, I did notice that Henry's gaze often lingered in my direction, and it worried me. I noticed that his eyes lingered on several of the serving wenches and I guessed that my son was busy sowing his seed; I just hoped that he was not going to try to use his charms on me.

This was exactly what I thought he was going to try, when about a week after he arrived, I heard his footsteps catching up to me, as I walked along the stone-covered tunnel that was used by the servants.

"Jenny...Jenny...wait, I need to talk with you." I had no need to turn around, to know that Henry was behind me. I had known by the sound of his footsteps, long before he had said a word. "Yes, master..." I said as I turned to him. "I wanted to ask you something...do you mind if I walk with you a while?" "As you wish..." I muttered, not knowing how I would be able deny his request.

We walked in an awkward silence for a few strides, our footsteps echoing on the stones. "I know what you are, Jenny."

I was stunned at his words, not knowing if he meant that he knew I was a vampire, or he knew I was his mother. "I am not sure what you mean..." I whispered, staring towards the floor, not daring to look up into his eyes. "I know what you are...I thought, at first, that my father had sent you to protect me...but now I am not sure...because, well... we look alike!"

He stopped walking, and I had no choice but to stop also. I turned towards him and lifted my eyes to look into his. "We share the same eyes, Jenny...even Jane noticed it...My mother died giving birth to me, but it has crossed my mind that she may have borne others, are you my sister Jenny?"

They had told him that I had died! I wanted to scream at him, to tell him who I was. I searched for words to form some sort of explanation, but my mind was blank, and my mouth could form no words. "I know you are a vampire, Jenny...I have lived amongst them so many years, I could not fail to know...but I need to know...are we kin?" "No... No..." Suddenly I had found my voice, but the truth was that I did not want to lie to him. I did not want to pretend that I did not exist. I wanted him to know that I was his mother and that I loved him. "If your father knew I was here he would kill me,"

I said in a surprisingly calm voice, although in truth, I was afraid of his reaction to what I had to say. "My name is Gwen...and I am your mother!" I whispered. "But you cannot be...it is not possible... I was told my mother had died." "No, Henry...no... Whoever told you that told you a falsehood...the reason why we share the same eyes is because..." I knelt down at his feet and looked up into his face, "The reason is because I am your mother..."

Chapter Eighteen

We talked for hours. I told of him of my parents and of my brothers, of his father Tom, and his family. I explained how I tried to take him away from Matilda and Robert, and of how I was banished for doing so. By the end of our discussion, he was in no doubt of the fact that I was his mother, but I could see confusion and doubt shadow his face, and so taking his hand I said, "What will you do?"

He abruptly pulled his hand from mine, and rubbed his forehead with his hand, in a sign I had come to recognize in him as a sign of frustration.

"What can I do? I will not betray you, how could I? However, I will not betray the people I have loved, and will always love, and who are, to me my mother and father. It is my duty to fulfill my father's wish, and I will fulfill that duty." His voice sounded callous and hard, and I knew he meant what he said.

"But you can remain human," in a voice that begged, "You do not need to become an ungodly creature like us...your children, they can remain human...you can be immortal through your descendants...that is the way it should be!" "Ah, but life is not so simple," he said, and after a long pause he looked into my eyes and said, "And I wish it...I want to turn...I am sorry that you do not agree...but it is my wish."

I wanted to shake him, to scream and shout, to demand he obey me, but it would have been a useless exercise, and so I said, my voice flat and void of emotion. "I vowed I would kill Matilda...I vowed I would take her life the day that you became a vampire." Henry said, in a voice that held conviction, "I cannot accept that...she is my mother...the only mother I have ever known...and I will, if the need should arise, avenge her death."

I turned away from him. I had my answer, I would never, in his eyes, be his mother. That special place in his heart was for Matilda and Matilda alone. I wanted to kill her! I wanted to rip her heart from her body and pierce it with a stake. Just as my own heart was pierced and broken from the pain of bitter rejection. As I turned back towards him, I knew, my eyes had glazed in an opaque stare, and my teeth had grown into pointed fangs, but he did not back away from me.

"So be it..." I growled, trying desperately to regain my composure. "I will not harm Matilda...but I will ask this of you. I ask that I can watch the ceremony of your rebirth into that of a vampire...and I ask to know the children of my child, for I know they are due to be born in the first days of November, a few weeks before you change."

His eyes never left my face; he was, I knew, trying to figure out if I was trying to trick him, and if I would, contrary to my words, try to kill Matilda the day of his rebirth.

"You give your word that you will not harm my mother?" he whispered. "Yes," I answered without hesitation. "I will allow you to see the girl...but I cannot agree to my son...my father will not allow it."

I wanted to demand to see my grandson, but I knew that I would in all likelihood be denied both if I disagreed. "You give me your word...son, Henry?" His face flushed at the sound of my words, but I was not sure if the cause was from pleasure at hearing my words or from anger. "Yes...I will give you my word, but for now you must disappear...my father will join us soon, and I am sure that you have no wish to see him?"

I nodded, placed the small bundle of clothes I had held the whole time we talked to the ground, and after raising my hand and holding it gently against Henry's face, I said, "I will see you in

November, until then, take care, my son..."

Chapter Nineteen

The days passed slowly after I left Whitehall. I missed Jane, but more so I missed Henry, and found I fought a constant battle with myself not to return to the palace, and shout *Robert be damned*! But, of course, I did not return, I wanted to be part of my granddaughter's life, and in order to ensure that I was, I needed, for the time being, to stay away.

I had rejoined my party of servants, and we traveled to a small inn about three miles south of Vanike Manor. It was ideal, close enough for me to travel to the manor, but far enough away so that it would be unlikely that I would to run into anyone I knew.

I had taken, once more, to waylaying rich strangers on the road and relieving them of their sovereigns and jewels. Although I was wealthy, I knew that I would always be in need of gold, I needed to be able to flee at the drop of a hat, and it cost a fortune to keep my band of servants. In truth, it was more than that. I needed to keep active, to throw my mind into the pursuit of prey, and forget about my son and Jane.

The spring passed and summer descended with a cloying heat. I had heard via my adventures on the road that my son and Jane had wed in June. The rich men I waylaid told me of the fanfare that surrounded the wedding, as I stole their wealth and their blood. They told of how beautiful the bride looked, but how none had outshone Queen Bess, and of how many of the guests had been startled to see Bess dressed like a bride in white, her gown studded with sparkling diamonds.

I listened intently, encouraging my prey to enlighten me with their thoughts and recollections. I pictured Henry dancing elegantly with the Queen, and I felt jealousy and rage engulf me, for I had not been there, *the one person who should have been*, to watch my son in such splendor.

The weeks passed, and I simmered like a flaming fireball, fueled with rage and pain. I relived, with my prey, my son's wedding, dreaming that I had been there, wishing that my life had been different, and praying for time to hurry so that I could see my family once more.

I am ashamed to admit that I acted without dignity or compassion at this time in my life. I drank from those I waylaid, too deeply, leaving them weak and sick. I sometimes took delight in torturing them with bites and knife cuts, and then leaving them to wander the night with no gold, and no knowledge of who or where they were. I took joy in bewitching them into forgetting their past, but what I enjoyed the most was taking away their memories of my son's wedding. I wanted them to forget it, to feel excluded, as I did, and so I took my revenge and jealousy out on poor unsuspecting travelers.

My summer of cruelty turned into an autumn of hell. I grew impatient, and so once again, the travelers of the road suffered. I know not how many people I slaughtered, nor how many I left along the roadside, to die without pity, a slow agonizing death. I killed, maimed, and slaughtered like a demon possessed. In truth, I become the depraved animal I despised, and hypocrisy mingled with my shame and anger in an explosion of violence. I was so young in mind, and I did not know, not then, that I rebelled against the fact that my son had rejected me. He had chosen Matilda over me and I had promised not to take my revenge. Instead, my wrath, the wrath I wanted to direct towards Matilda and Robert, was released upon my innocent victims.

My rampage ended on a blustery All Hallows Eve. I had returned from my hunt for victims, when on entering the inn, the innkeeper shouted towards me, his voice cheerful and happy. "Will you not share a mug of ale with us mistress?...Tonight our lord was blessed with two newborns, a girl and a boy, it is said. They be born on All Hallows Eve...and it is our blessings they need...it is a curse to be born on such a night, is it not, my lady?"

I directed my joy towards the innkeeper in the form of a radiant smile. My grandchildren had arrived, and I would now make my way to Vanike Manor to greet my granddaughter. I turned to leave, but the innkeeper once more called out, "Mistress, will you not drink to their health with us?" "Yes of course, my good man," I shouted, striding towards him, "Your best wine, man, for the whole inn." I took the first goblet of wine, drank it down, and shouted, "*Long may they live and with God's will they will be blessed.*" I slammed the goblet down on the table, and shouted as I made my way to the inn door, "*Drink to their health, all of you...and innkeeper, I will settle with you tomorrow.*" I ran from the inn doorway, vaulted on my unsaddled horse's back, and galloped towards Vanike.

Chapter Twenty

I rode my horse like a demon possessed, towards Vanike. I knew not how I would make my entry into the manor, and at that moment, I did not care. I was determined to hold my grandchild, no matter what or whom I had to cross to achieve it.

On arrival to the manor, I stood in the shadow of the trees, watching the comings and goings of the servants. It struck me that I probably would not be noticed if I slipped inside the manor, kept my head down, and took the servants' back stairs.

Pulling my cloak hood around my face, I walked to the log pile, which was stacked next to the doorway. I took several of the logs and casually made my way to the entrance. As I predicted, I walked unnoticed through the opening, servants were running back and forth, too busy to notice a woman carrying logs.

I hastily made my way through the curtain and up the servants' stairs. On reaching the small narrow corridor that led to the bedchambers I realised, quite stupidly, that I did not know where Jane and the babies were located.

I tried to listen for the soft mewing sound of newborn babies, but the manor was full of many noises, and I was unable to distinguish any individual sounds. I slapped my leg in anger and frustration, and it was just at that moment that I heard the sound of soft footfall behind me. I turned quickly, and gasped; standing in front of me, in all of his glory, was Robert, his eyes blazing, his fangs poised.

I felt dizzy from the range of emotions that spun inside of me. It all came back instantly, the lust, the want, and above all else the love I felt for him. "So you return, Gwen," he said in a deep growl. I could not speak, my mouth had lost the ability to work, and I just stood, mute, staring at him.

"Henry said you would return, but I wagered you would not...it looks like I am the loser of that bet." Again he paused, his eyes raking up and down my body hungrily. "I told you never to return, Gwen...but then you never did listen to me, did you?" Finally I found my voice, albeit that it sounded very shaky and nervous. "I have only returned to see my granddaughter, Robert. I will leave as quietly as I have arrived, I am not here for war ..." Robert threw his head back, a hearty laugh vibrating in his throat.

"Oh but you are still so arrogant, Gwen! I told you I would kill you; remember? I am almost certain that the act does not involve walking away from anyone or anything." "Can I see my granddaughter first?" I asked, pulling my body up straight and into my full height, my eyes held his steadily, and I refused to cower.

"So much bravery in that little body, Gwen...is it any wonder that I wanted you to be the mother of my son and heir?" he whispered, almost as if he was talking to himself.

"Henry told me of your bargain..." He paused again, and then continued, "I will allow you to see the girl, she is weak and will probably not survive...but the boy is mine." I bowed my head in acceptance. I had known that I would not be able to see my grandson, and although it angered me, I knew better than to push Robert for that which he was unwilling to give.

"But I will not allow you to witness Henry's rebirth." I started to protest, but he held his hand up to silence me. "No, Gwen, I do not trust you, you are not one to hold to a bargain, and I have a feeling that you will try to stop the ceremony in some way."

"But..." I tried again to protest. "There are no buts, Gwen...I command you to stay away from here; if you do not then I will do what I promised you I would, on that night nearly seventeen years ago. *Do you understand me, Gwen?*"

I knew he meant what he said, and so I let my eyes drop, and whispered, "Yes, Robert...I will do as you say." He did not comment on my answer, but simply beckoned me to follow him, and made his way quickly to my old bedchamber.

A small wooden crib rested by the bed, a woman, obviously the wet nurse, sat on a stool beside it, rocking it gently from time to time. There was no sign of my grandson, Jane, or Henry.

"Why is she alone, away from her brother and mother?" I asked. "She is weak...it is better for her here." Robert's voice was hard and rough sounding. I did not comment on what he said, but I knew that his response was false; it felt as if they had thrown her away, before they had even given her a chance.

I walked over to the crib, pulled the woollen blankets back, and looked into the face of my blood. She was so small, and all alone. Her skin felt, to my gentle touch, like the finest cream silk, and her features were so tiny and perfectly formed.

She was the smallest baby I had ever seen, and I thought, at first, that this was why they had given her up to die. Reaching over I lifted her gently from the crib, and pulled her to my chest. Her eyes opened wide, and they were the same blue as her father's and mine.

"What is her name?" I asked in a whisper, not wanting to startle her. "We have not named her," Robert said, not bothering to lower his voice. "She will not survive, Gwen."

There was something so wrong with his words. I knew that Robert's blood could heal almost any ailment, so why did he not feed her, that which would make her live? Moreover, the child's heartbeat was strong, she was a fighter, and I believed she would live. I did not trust Robert's words, there was another reason other than he believed she was too weak, and I would find out why, or die trying.

I forged a look of sadness onto my features, and looking up at him said, "I believe, like you, Robert that she shall not live long...but we all deserve a name, do we not? I shall think of her always as a white rose, perfect and pure."

Robert walked away from my side and waited by the door. "It is time for you to take your leave, Gwen," he said abruptly.

I lowered my lips to Rose, and biting the inside of my mouth, I quickly pushed the tip of my blood-covered tongue into her perfectly formed mouth. I knew my blood did not hold the healing properties of Robert's, but I hoped it would sustain her until I returned.

I placed her back in the crib, gave her one last kiss, making sure her lips held no trace of my blood, and walked towards Robert. We quickly made our way in silence down the servants' staircase, through the great hall, and out to where I had tethered my horse.

"I take it you will not be back, Gwen?" Robert asked as he watched me hoist myself up on to the horse's back. "I gave you my word, Robert," I replied abruptly. Then, in an attempt to sound gracious, I said, "There is no point in me coming back, but thank you, Robert...for allowing me to see her."

Robert visibly relaxed and whispered, "It was the least I could do, Gwen, and I hope life treats you well." I smiled at him briefly, whipped my horse around, and galloped in the direction of the inn without looking back.

I had lied, I had every intention of coming back for Henry's rebirth, for I had a feeling that the ill treatment of Rose was somehow connected to that ceremony. I had decided that I would return on the last day of November, the birthday of my son, and protect my granddaughter, whatever the cost.

Chapter Twenty-One

Over the next four weeks, I planned for our escape. I suspected that Rose was to be included in Henry's rebirth ceremony, and I had begun to think that they intended to sacrifice her. I was not, under any circumstance, going to allow that to happen.

Daily I waylaid strangers on their travels, but I had stopped killing. My mind was now set on rescuing the child of my blood, and murder was not part of that rescue.

When the eve of my son's birthday arrived, I was ready. I had forged a disguise, it was only small changes in appearance, but I was sure that it would be enough to allow me to enter Vanike without notice.

I lightened my hair and eyebrows with urine in the weeks leading up to the ceremony. It was the most foul of experiences, but it worked, and my hair turned the colour of copper leaves floating on an autumn morn. I braided my hair tight to my scalp, a style I had never worn before, and I blackened under my eyes with charcoal, which helped to age me by several years. I also used rags to bulk out my figure to that of a woman at least ten years older, the rags also helped to hide the wooden stakes tied to my body...

I had organized my party of servants so that they had already made haste to Dover, and would wait for me in a small inn on a cove near Dover's white cliffs. The very same ship I had crossed from France in, awaited my boarding at the cove, we would cross the English Channel to Calais, and from there I would travel to wherever I wished.

The risks were high, and the difficulty would lie in snatching Rose and escaping unscathed, I knew there was a very good chance that we would both die in the endeavor.

I had timed my arrival well and when I arrived, the great hall was full of vampires. I did not recognise many faces from the crowd, and I knew if this was the case, then they would likewise not recognise me.

I made my way slowly towards the front of the rabble. Not close enough that I was able to be observed by Robert, Henry, or Matilda, but close enough to make my move when the time came. Matilda, as always, shone brightly in a beguiling gown of emerald green velvet, threaded with gold thread, and sparkling with diamonds. Her eyes sparkled like the jewels she wore, and I felt my hatred of her build afresh, as I watched her move around with catlike grace. Robert stood on the other side of the hall, his presence godly, overpowering, and all-consuming. He did not need jewels or fine clothes to gain attention, his being naturally drew admirers, as a candle welcomes moths. Henry, my son, stood in between them. He shone as greatly as those at his sides, and I did not doubt that he would fulfill the destiny that Robert had predicted for him.

I watched as they prepared themselves for the ceremony, which would see Robert with the son of his and Matilda's blood. They had fed Henry from before he was born, via me, the vessel, with both of their blood, and his rebirth would be born from both of their blood.

The atmosphere in the hall started to change, and excitement charged the air. Robert stepped forward, his hands held high.

"Today you will witness the rebirth of my son, Henry," he shouted to the now silent crowd. *"He will become a great prince, the first true prince of the vampires; his destiny will begin!"*

The vampires cheered heartily to the sound of Robert's voice. I ignored their cheers; to me they were no better than animals following the pack leader. It was at this point that I noticed Matilda turn and walk towards the roaring fire. She swiftly bent down and then straightening up, walked towards Henry with a small bundle in her arms, she then placed it in on the floor in front of him.

"The child of our son," she shouted to the crowd, *"The pure blood of innocence will give our son strength, her blood will power his reign, and her kin sacrifice will be his life's blood."*

Rose was to be Henry's first taste of blood, and his first kill as a vampire! For the first time in a very long time, I felt vomit fill my throat in disgust; swallowing it down, I moved forward. I knew that I needed to act quickly, because Henry was now kneeling behind Rose, his head flung back in preparation for the slicing of his throat and his death.

I pulled the stake out from under my skirt, and before anyone could stop me, I lunged at Matilda, the stake in my hand pierced her body, and her scream echoed with horrific clarity around the great hall. I had very little time and so I ran towards Rose and quickly snatched her into my arms, but I was too late, Robert was already by my side.

I thought he would kill us both, but he ignored us, and he walked past us as if we were not even present. His intention was clear; he wanted to reach Matilda's side. When he did, he fell to the floor and pulled her now aged and rotting body into his arms.

His voice rang out around the hall in a language that sounded as ancient as time, I did not understand him, but I was sure that I was not alone in my bewilderment.

His voice echoed repeatedly. Agony, deep and raw, resonated within the sound. The pain in his voice clenched at my heart, it was the sound of a broken but enraged animal. The sound suddenly awoke within me the awareness that I must escape before his anger swept the hall like an avenging demon.

I scurried quickly towards the doorway. Not looking into the faces of the vampires surrounding me, as I was sure if I did, then they would be aware of our escape and Rose and I would be torn limb from limb.

I had just about reached the entrance when what can only be described as a howl, although the force of it caused the stone of the manor to shake around me, and was unlike any sound I heard before or since, vibrated in the air. *"MARRRRRRRRRRRRRRRRRYYYYYY YYYYYYYYYYYYY"*

His voice repeated, piercing my mind and delaying my progress, I was confused, for he shouted 'Mary', not 'Matilda'.

Disorientated by the sound of his voice vibrating inside my skull, I made the mistake of looking back towards him. His eyes shone like the burning sun into mine, his wrath was such that I felt I could feel it scorch me from across the hall.

I watched, mesmerized, as he moved with

great speed towards my son. He then grabbed Henry's head in his hands, and pulling it back towards he twisted his head as if it were no more than a twig in his fingers. Robert sunk his teeth into his own wrist, which enabled his blood to flow freely. He then held his wrist to Henry's mouth, and in doing so, completed Henry's rebirth. Robert's blood had slid down my son's throat in the moment of death, Henry was now a vampire.

Robert had watched me throughout the whole of the quickly performed ceremony, but not once did he move towards me. Even now, I do not know how, but I somehow managed to find the strength to turn away from his gaze and stumble out through the doorway. I tied Rose, in her blanket, tightly around me, vaulted on my horse and took off, away from Vanike, Robert, and my son, at a raging gallop.

I was expecting at any time during our journey, to feel the touch of Robert's hands on my back. Although I did hear for the first few miles of our journey his high-pitched, terrifying screams of rage, vibrate through the air.

I rode through the night, stealing a fresh horse when the one I rode tired. I never stopped for very long, always afraid that Robert would swoop in and strike me down. Rose slept for the whole of the journey, her little body snuggled into mine, her small hand gripping tightly at my breast.

We arrived at the white cliffs just as the sun lit the day. And it was a beautiful but crisp, cold, and frosty English morning. Wearily I climbed aboard the ship and handed Rose to the wet nurse I had hired in preparation for her care. I needed to rest, and to feel the warmth of sweet, salty blood, lovingly coat my throat, and in doing so, it would restore my strength and power.

Beckoning one of the rough looking sailors towards me, I drank from him, and felt his masculine power, warm my cold and tired body. My eyes closed, and I felt the soft arms of sleep start to engulf me. It was at that moment, as I drifted on the outskirts of sleep, that the thought returned, and my eyes flew open.

I had puzzled, as I rode like a demon through the night, as to why Robert did not kill us. He could have quite easily, I was in no doubt about that, but why had he not done so? I tried to find the answer, but it would not come at first, but as the night wore on, and as I constantly looked over my shoulder, the answer came to me.

Robert's punishment was to ensure that I never found peace. My sanity would always be tested, by the constant need to look over my shoulder, the constant need to run, and the constant thought that one day he would take all I held dear, take it away from me and destroy it. He knew that I would live with the knowledge that my son hated me, and one day, be it even in four or five hundred years, he would find me, and with Robert's help, he would avenge Matilda's death.

I closed my eyes, but as I drifted into a restless sleep, I knew that I had won the battle, but I had not won the war, and my fight had only just begun.

About the author

Having run a successful garden centre then a floristry business, Charmain Mitchell never really had time to concentrate on her passion for writing.

Throughout her life, Charmain has wanted to become an author, but family and business commitments stood in the way and her writing consisted of a few short stories on the rare occasion that she had time to write them.

In late 2012 a freak accident finally allowed time for Charmain to indulge in her passion for writing. She says of this;

"Then a few weeks ago I fell over whilst trying to catch chickens and ended up breaking my ankle! Quite a comical way to break your ankle - I know; especially when I have kept horses for the majority of my life and have never yet broken any bones where they are concerned!

Suddenly I had six clear weeks in which I wouldn't be able to move very well? Help! How was I going to cope with doing zilch for that long? Then I thought, maybe I should do a bit of writing, and that is what I did, and the strange thing is, is that I haven't been able to stop since!"

She says of her writing

"I love writing, it is truly my passion! I love the way that through words I can make people think and feel differently, feel passion, sometimes pain, and get totally lost in my words. I love the fact that a brilliant writer will live forever, and will in some way influence generations to come. Is it not marvelous that we can still look back to writing from over two thousand years ago and believe in it and still learn from it?

The human imagination is a wondrous thing, it creates and then brings to life stories on a screen, and sometimes we believe in these stories so much that they become our passion. I'm talking about for instance: the Lord of the Rings, Harry Potter, and Star Wars etc... I think we actually forget sometimes that all of these stories were started with a simple idea on a piece of paper, and they grew to be something that some of us forget started from the author's imagination".

Charmain Mitchell lives in a semi-rural village on the south coast of the UK with her four children, husband, two cats, and countless chickens.

Excerpt: short story from '**The Lust for Blood**'

A Passion for Death

Nicola read her horoscope and sighed. Not one mention of love, or the hope of it. Although she didn't know why she bothered looking, because even if her horoscope did shout out 'Great love on the way for Leos!' the words never ran true, and she had never yet bumped into her 'great love'.

For some reason she was drawn to wanting to know the future, if it wasn't horoscopes then it was tarot cards, palmistry, or mediums, and sometimes even witchcraft. She loved everything to do with the supernatural, and had hundreds of books on the art of fortune telling, spells, and Wicca, but nothing she did seemed to get her the one thing she desired - someone she could love and who would love her just as much in return.

She didn't understand why she found it so difficult to attract male attention. She wasn't ugly and although she wasn't gorgeous either, she knew she didn't look bad. She always termed herself as average. She had an average face with no huge or ugly features, but then again no beautiful features either. She had average mousey brown hair, which was cut into an average shoulder-length bob. An average figure, nothing to write home about; but then again nothing to complain about either. Nicola was an average person, and she admitted to herself that this was her downfall - she just did not stand out from the crowd. She blended in so much that no one saw or noticed her, and no one can find attractive, what cannot be seen.

Nicola had tried every possible means to try and look different, and had even had her hair colored platinum blonde at one point. She did not, however, succeed in getting herself noticed, but she did succeed in making herself feel very uncomfortable, and had at the time taken to wearing a woolly hat on every time she popped to the shops. Finally, after two weeks of walking around in the middle of an unexpected hot English summer with what looked like a tea cozy stuck atop of her head, she decided to return to her average mousey brown colour.

Having been an only child of an old-fashioned couple who had unexpectedly had a child in their late forties, both being dead for many years, Nicola at forty-five years old was alone in the world, with just her job at the local library to keep her company. It was a combination of all of these factors that led Nicola into the world of the supernatural, and ultimately into the performing of spells, love potions, and minor black magic.

Nicola's hobby became a passion and ultimately after a while her passion turned into an obsession. Nicola scoured bookshops and online stores in pursuit of better and more daring black magic. She would find love; she decided, even if it killed her, or condemned her to hell in the process!

It was because of this obsessive pursuit that Nicola came across a book on eBay called 'My Secret Spells'. A first print book, written in the late eighteen hundreds, Nicola was ecstatic and knew instantly that she must have this rare artifact. Deciding that she must have the book, Nicola recklessly made bids on the book, even when the total figure reached very many thousands, and nearly all of her savings. She did not care! The spell book, she knew, was the key to unlocking the love that lay dormant deep within her heart.

The day the book arrived by post, Nicola acted like a kid in a sweet shop, and on unwrapping the book, danced around her house with the book outstretched in her arms. She then sat down and read, in her haste not noticing the delightful old smell of a book that had survived for over two hundred years.

The book contained many love spells and potions, but all the spells needed rare ingredients and tools, all of which would take her many months to gather; all of them, it seemed, except for one very simple spell.

The spell simply needed a black pepper candle, a bowl of water, a mirror, and a drop of her own blood. She also needed to recite a Latin spell at the stroke of midnight and chant the words:

'De Profundis, abyssus abyssum invocat, homo mortuus resurrectionem, do ut facias ad extremum amate, orta recens quam pura nites!' Nicola had no idea what the incantation meant. She did not care. All she knew was that the spell was entitled 'Rekindling of a man's Passion and Love' and that was all Nicola needed or wanted to know.

Gathering up a beeswax candle, wick and copious amounts of black pepper, (Nicola congratulated herself on having several tubs of the spice in the cupboard); she started to make the black pepper candle.

Although Nicola did curse profoundly at the amount of sneezing that grinding up such a huge amount of black pepper caused her. Not once did she wonder why she needed to use the spice, and even if she had of known that the spice was also called 'Spirit', she would never have stopped to wonder what relevance that held in such a spell. Her only aim at that time was to prepare and perform the spell; the consequences that might arise from doing so never once entered her head.

Placing the candle in the fridge to harden, Nicola got ready for bed. She could hardly wait for the following night to arrive, and willed herself to sleep early in order to make the night pass and the time for performing the spell to approach quicker.

The next day passed the same as any other in Nicola's life. She got up, ate a bowl of porridge and made her way to work. Louisa and John, the two other librarians, greeted her on her entry to the library, and she them in return and then, just like any other day, Nicola settled down to work. Nicola never stopped for a lunch break; and simply shook her head without looking up when John asked her if she would like to join him at the pub across the road.

The fact of the matter was that John asked Nicola to join him for lunch at least once a week, and if she had just taken the time to notice, she would have seen a man besotted standing in front of her. Nicola thought his request was just a friendly one, she had never contemplated that he could be interested in her in a romantic sense, had decided long ago that he was far above her in the dating stakes. Nicola instead decided to block him out, and so never saw the wistful gaze he often bestowed in her direction or the softening in his manner when he talked to her, and instead she retreated further into her obsession, not seeing that the love she sought was already within easy reach.

After work had finished for the day, Nicola hurried home and set to work preparing everything she needed for the spell. A full-length mirror hung on the wall in her bedroom, and she decided this was where she was going to perform the incantation and placed a bowl of water, the candle, matches, the spell book, and a small knife in which to draw blood from her own hand, in front of the mirror. Nicola then ran a hot bath, perfuming the water with a concoction of rose water and combining the essence with an incantation, she had read in one of her other spell books that this would make her irresistible to the opposite sex.

Several times Nicola topped up the hot water, enabling her to luxuriate in the bath for just over two hours. She repeated the Latin incantation she needed to chant whilst performing the spell.

"De Profundis, abyssus abyssum invocat, homo mortuus resurrectionem, do ut facias ad extremum amate, orta recens quam pura nites!"

Several times she wondered why the word 'resurrectionem' cropped up in the spell, a word which she had recognized has being the word 'resurrection', but after deciding that she didn't want to face the reality of the meaning, carried on with her chanting regardless of any doubts.

Finally, the time had come to perform the spell. At ten minutes to midnight, Nicola knelt before the mirror in the darkness, dressed in a flowing white satin nightgown. The only light came from the ghostly shine of her mobile phone screen as she counted down the minutes in anticipation. At precisely one minute to twelve, Nicola picked up the matches, lit the black pepper candle, and turned off her mobile phone. Picking up the small silver penknife, she started to recant the spell in a tiny whisper, and whilst looking deeply into the mirror drew the knife across her palm, letting her blood flow freely into the bowl of water beneath.

"De Profundis, abyssus abyssum invocat, homo mortuus resurrectionem, do ut facias ad extremum amate, orta recens quam pura nites!"

She whispered repeatedly. Nicola then placed the knife on the floor beside the bowl of water, picked up the candle and tilted it so that some of the wax dropped into the water and mixed with her blood.

"De Profundis, abyssus abyssum invocat, homo mortuus resurrectionem, do ut facias ad extremum amate, orta recens quam pura nites!"

Nicola stared without blinking into the mirror, at first not noticing the black shadow growing in the depth of the room behind her. It was only when the candle flickered that she noticed the growing shadow materializing into the form of the man.

"De Profundis, abyssus abyssum invocat, homo mortuus resurrectionem, do ut facias ad extremum amate, orta recens quam pura nites!"

Her voice grew stronger and louder, her eyes wider. She did not notice, but her whole being trembled in fear and anticipation. The shadow moulded into the contours of a man of large, but perfect stature, his handsome features slowly came into soft focus, and then grew sharper and solid. Suddenly Nicola could see that he wore a Victorian suit and a long black cape that hung gracefully from his broad shoulders. The very last thing to become clear was his eyes, they shone like chips of perfect emeralds, glistening and hard, and in that moment, Nicola knew she was lost forever.

"You called for me, my love?" The man said. The chanting died on Nicola's lips. As if in a dream; Nicola arose from the floor, turned, and ran willingly into his arms.

To Nicola it seemed as if she had known him all her life, his movements, the tilt of head, everything was so familiar. "You will do anything I wish?" he asked of her.
"Oh yes," she replied, "Anything, I am yours forever." He laughed at her words, his eyes reflected the flame of the candle, and it seemed for a moment that they were alight with an orange dancing flame. "Oh my love, you have no idea how long I've waited for you!" "I do, my love, oh I do, and I have waited for you also!" Nicola cried breathlessly.

He pushed her back onto the bed, his hands caressing her soft rose-scented skin, and although no man had ever touched her before, Nicola melted to his touch. He stripped the nightgown from her body and caressed her taut nipples with his cold lips. She pulled him towards her, wanting him to consume her, screaming in ecstasy when his body thrust deeply into hers.

When their lovemaking had finished Nicola watched him rise from the bed. A frown skipped across her brow in confusion because he was once more fully dressed, where just seconds before he was naked. Suddenly a thought crossed her mind and she giggled. "I don't know your name?" she said, blushing. "My name is John, although I am known as Jack." "Nice to meet you Jack....I am Nicola."

Jack smiled down at her. She blushed, shyness becoming apparent now that their passion had dwindled. Jack knelt down and picked the penknife off the floor, caressing it lovingly like an old friend.

"Did you stop to think what the words of the incantation meant, Nicola?" Jack asked, turning back towards her. "Um no.....not really!" Nicola answered truthfully, watching mesmerized as he still fingered the knife lovingly in his hands. "Shall I tell you?" he asked her, a quiver of a smile touching his lips. "Yes...Um yes please." Nicola was starting to feel scared. The hairs on the back of her neck had risen whilst watching him finger the knife, and a jolt of fear had spiraled down her backbone when she saw his cruel smile.

"De Profundis, abyssus abyssum invocat, homo mortuus resurrectionem, do ut facias ad extremum amate, orta recens quam pura nites!"

He shouted, leaning closer to Nicola over the bed, loving the fear that crept into her eyes.

"De Profundis, abyssus abyssum invocat, homo mortuus resurrectionem, do ut facias ad extremum amate, orta recens quam pura nites! Means the following my love Out of the depths of despair, hell calls hell, dead man resurrection, I give to you so that you may do to the extreme that what you love, newly risen how brightly you shine!"

Nicola sat up in the bed, pulling the sheet up with her in order to cover her breasts, and suddenly she cowered under his stare. "Do you remember what the spell was called?" Nicola did not answer him, but simply nodded her head. "Oh come, my dear, don't be shy....We are lovers, are we not? Tell me, Nicola, what was the spell called?"

Nicola tried to answer but fear had stolen her voice, and the only sound that materialized from her throat was an anguished croak. "Oh dear, I've frightened you, my love......Very well I will tell you...The spell was called 'Rekindling of a man's passion and love'!" He looked at her, his face and manner mocking. "You have no doubt by now have realized that you have resurrected my spirit?" Nicola nodded again, fear etched into every feature.

He sat down on the edge of the bed, taking her shaking hand into his, and continued softly, "Do you know what my passion was when I lived, Nicola? The passion and love you rekindled?" His eyes sought hers, evil and amusement radiating from them in green and blue sparks.

"Oh dear, my love, you seem to have lost your power of speech?...Come tell me, take a guess?" His hand held hers tightly, biting into her skin. "No...I don't know!" Nicola whispered. Leaning closer, Jack whispered into her ear, "I loved to kill, my love, to taste and smell the sweet stench of flowing blood....What do you say to that?"

Nicola tried to kick and scream, but Jack was too strong, and held her as if she was no more than a child.

"Oh darling, don't scream.....It will be all over soon, and besides I haven't told you everything." Nicola stopped struggling and looked into his eyes, she knew he was going to kill her, she could see the excitement in his face, and the vibrancy rising in his body, she knew with certainty that it was pointless to fight.

"I lived not far from here, a few streets away in fact, but I loved one place above all others in London......I loved Whitechapel!" He laughed when he noticed the comprehension dawn in Nicola's face.

"Yes, Whitechapel was my first love. You see even though I had killed and murdered many times before, it was in Whitechapel that my skill was recognized, and it was in Whitechapel that I gained the name that still strikes fear in many today....My name, my love, although I have a sneaky feeling that you already know it...MY NAME IS JACK....JACK THE RIPPER!"

Nicola knew what was going to happen, and even though she saw the glint of the knife blade slice through the air, it still came as a shock to her when he plunged it deep into the point just below her sternum. She did not really feel any pain as he sliced down wards, nor when he pulled back her skin and pulled out her intestines, although by this time she was floating in the air above them both. She watched him slice her breast from her body, hold it up in triumph, and with a manic laugh start to suck on her dead nipple. The last thing Nicola saw before her life faded into nothingness was Jack bending down, licking at the open gash where once her breast had been. His handsome face distorted by a crazed disgusting lust, and an evil smile twisting his perfect mouth.

When Jack had finished his work, Nicola's bedroom resembled the slaughter room of the local abattoir. Her intestines hung artistically over the lampshade, her breasts placed like ornaments on her dressing table, and her internal organs were scattered like a shrine around her slaughtered body.

Jack, however, was not satisfied. It was true that he had sated a lust that had built over the last one hundred years, but there was no satisfaction from killing a woman like Nicola! There was no fight! She had simply accepted her fate, and that was not really to his taste. He had realized long ago where to go to get a woman who would fight for survival, a woman who had lived hard and would die harder! He needed a prostitute, and preferably one from Whitechapel.

Jack was about to leave, but just before he glided soundlessly onto the streets of London in pursuit of his perfect prey, an amusing idea crossed his mind. Dipping his finger into Nicola's congealing blood he turned to the magnolia and blood spattered wall, and wrote a message in his elegant slanting handwriting.

'I'm back' J.T.R'

Other books available by the author

Vampire – In the Beginning: The first book in the Vampire series, the tale of how Gwen first became a vampire.

The lust for Blood, thirteen gruesome horror stories (warning very graphic).

Look out for these titles in the following year:

The Lust for Blood 2 – The supernatural files.

The first in a new series of books – Death whisper (Mary Howard, supernatural mysteries series)

Vampire – The Quest for Truth (third book in the 'Vampire' series).

To discover more about the author and books available visit:

http://www.charmainmariemitchell.com